"Just for tonight," she said, hating that she had to say it, but knowing she did. Because she knew for certain that there could be no romantic future for them.

She loved him. She was certain of it now. She had for a long time—possibly for most of the seven years she'd known him. It had been a slow thing, working its way into her system bit by bit. With every smile, every touch.

And he didn't love her. Looking at him now, she saw the light in his eyes wasn't anything deeper than lust. But if that was all she could have she would take it, and she wouldn't think about the wisdom of it, or the consequences.

If he wanted her right now, then she'd take it. Because she was staring hard into a Zack-free future, and she would rather have all of him tonight, and carry the memory with her, than be nothing more than his trusty sidekick forever, standing by watching while he married another woman. Watching him make a life with someone else, someone he didn't even love, while her heart splintered into tiny pieces with every beat.

"One night," she repeated. "Here. Away from reality. Away from work and home. Because...we can't keep going on like this. It can't be healthy."

ONE NIGHT IN...

Let Mills & Boon® Modern™ Romance
whisk you away on the jet-set trip of a lifetime!

From the heat of the desert to the cosmopolitan flair
of Madrid, from sultry Brazil to opulent London,
seduction is a language that knows no bounds!

Real heroes know that
sometimes actions speak louder than words...

Meet the lucky heroines who discover this first-hand
in these dramatic stories of one night of incredible
passion, and wherever it leads...

One Night In...

A night with these men is never enough!

ONE NIGHT
IN PARADISE

BY
MAISEY YATES

First published in Great Britain 2012
by Mills & Boon, an imprint of Harlequin (UK) Limited.
Harlequin (UK) Limited, Eton House, 18-24 Paradise Road,
Richmond, Surrey TW9 1SR

© Maisey Yates 2012

ISBN: 978 0 263 22714 7

Harlequin (UK) policy is to use papers that are natural, renewable and recyclable products and made from wood grown in sustainable forests. The logging and manufacturing process conform to the legal environmental regulations of the country of origin.

Printed and bound in Great Britain
by CPI Antony Rowe, Chippenham, Wiltshire

Maisey Yates was an avid Mills & Boon® Modern™ Romance reader before she began to write them. She still can't quite believe she's lucky enough to get to create her very own sexy alpha heroes and feisty heroines. Seeing her name on one of those lovely covers is a dream come true.

Maisey lives with her handsome, wonderful, diaper-changing husband and three small children across the street from her extremely supportive parents and the home she grew up in, in the wilds of Southern Oregon, USA. She enjoys the contrast of living in a place where you might wake up to find a bear on your back porch and then heading into the home office to write stories that take place in exotic urban locales.

Recent titles by the same author:

To my very best friend,
who I happened to be married to. Haven, I love you.

CHAPTER ONE

Clara Davis looked at the uneaten cake, still as pristine and pink as the bride had demanded, sitting on its pedestal. A very precarious pedestal that had taken a whole lot of skill to balance and get set up. Not to mention have delivered to the coast-side hotel that sat twenty miles away from her San Francisco kitchen.

Everything would have been perfect. The cake, the setting, the groom, well, he was beyond perfect, as usual. And everyone who had been invited had come.

There had been one key person missing, though. The bride had decided to skip the event. And without her, it made it sort of tricky to continue.

Clara eyed the cake and considered taking a slice for herself. She'd worked hard on it. No sense letting it go to waste.

She sighed. The cake wouldn't make the knot in her stomach go away. It wouldn't ease any of the sadness she felt. Nothing had been able to shake that feeling, not since the groom, who was now officially jilted, had announced the engagement in the first place.

Though, ironically, watching him get stood up at the altar hadn't made her feel any better. But how could it? She didn't like seeing Zack hurt. He was her business partner—more than that, he was her best friend. And also, yeah, the man who kept her awake some nights with the kinds of fantasies that did not bear rehashing in the light of day.

But secret fantasies aside, she hadn't really wanted the wedding to fall apart. Well, not this close to the actual ceremony. Or maybe she had wanted it. Maybe a small part of her had hoped this would be the outcome.

Maybe that was why she'd agreed to bake the cake. To stand by and watch Zack bind himself to another woman for the rest of his life. There wasn't really another sane reason for it.

She blew out a breath and walked out of the kitchen and into the massive, empty reception hall. Her heart hit hard against her breastbone when she saw Zack Parsons, coffee mogul, business genius and abandoned groom, standing near the window, looking out at the beach, the sun casting an orange glow on his face and bleeding onto the pristine white of his tuxedo shirt.

He looked different, for just a moment. Leaner. Harder than she was used to seeing him. His tie was draped over his shoulders, his jacket a black puddle by his feet. He was leaning against the window, bracing himself on his forearm.

It shouldn't really shock her that after being left at the altar he looked stronger in a strange way.

"Hey," she said, her voice sounding too loud. Stupid in the empty room.

He turned, his gray eyes locking with hers, and she stopped breathing for a moment. He truly was the most beautiful man on the planet. Seven years of working with him on a daily basis should have taken some of the impact away. And some days she was able to ignore it, or at least sublimate it. But then there were other days when it hit her with the force of ten tons of bricks.

Today was one of those days.

"What kind of cake did I buy, Clara?" he asked, pushing off from the window and stuffing his hand into his pocket.

She forced herself to breathe. "The bottom tier was vanilla, with raspberry filling, per Hannah's instructions. And there was pink fondant. Which I hand-painted, by the way. But the vanilla cake in the middle was soaked in bourbon and honey. And not a single walnut on the whole cake. Because I know what you like."

"Good. Have someone wrap up the middle tier and send it to my house. And they can send Hannah her tier, too."

"You don't have to do that. You can throw it out."

"It's edible. Why would I throw it out?"

"Uh...because it was your wedding cake. For a wedding that didn't happen. For most people it might...take the sweet out of it."

He shrugged one shoulder. "Cake is cake."

She put her hand on her hip and affected a haughty expression, hoping to force a slight smile. "My cake is more than mere cake, but I get your point."

"We've made a fortune off your cakes, I'm aware of how spectacular they are."

"I know. But I can make a new cake. I can make a cake that says Condolences on Your Canceled Nuptials. We could put a man on top of it sitting in a recliner, watching sports on his flat-screen television, with no bride in sight."

The corner of his mouth lifted slightly and she felt a small bubbly sensation in her chest. As though a weight had just been removed.

"That won't be necessary."

"That could be a new thing we offer in the shops, Zack," she said, knowing business was his favorite topic, aborted wedding or no. "Little cupcakes for sad occasions."

"I'm not all that sad."

"You aren't?"

"I'm not heartbroken, if that's what you're wondering."

Clara frowned. "But you got left at the altar. Public humiliation is...well, it's never fun. I had something like that happen in high school when I got stood up by my date at a dance.

People pointed and laughed. I was humiliated. It was all very Carrie. Without the pig's blood or the mass murder."

"Not the highlight of my life, Clara, I'll admit." He swallowed. "Not the lowest point, either. I would have preferred for her to leave me before I was standing at the altar, with the preacher, in a tux, in front of nearly a thousand people, but I'm not exactly devastated."

"That's…well, that's good." Except it was sort of scary to know that he could be abandoned just before taking his vows and respond to it with an eerie calm. She reacted more strongly to a recipe that didn't pan out the way she wanted it to.

But then, Zack was always the one with the zenlike composure. When they'd first met, over a cupcake of all things, she'd been impressed by that right away. That and his beautiful eyes, but that was a different story.

She'd been working at a small bakery in the Mission District in San Francisco, and he'd been scoping out a new location for his local chain of coffee shops. He'd bought one of her peanut-butter-banana cupcakes, her experiment du jour. His reaction, like all of Zack's reactions, hadn't been overly demonstrative. But there had been a glint in his eye, a hint of that hard steel that lay just beneath the outer calm.

And he'd come back the next day, and the next. She'd never entertained, not for a moment, the idea that he'd been coming in to see her. It had been all about the cupcakes.

And then he'd offered her twice the money to come and work in his flagship shop, making the treats of her choice in his gorgeous, state-of-the-art kitchen. It had been the start of everything for her. At eighteen it had been a major break, and had allowed her to get out of her parents' house, something she'd been desperate to do.

In the years since, it had been a whole lot more than that.

Roasted's ten thousandth location had just opened, their first in Japan, and it was being hailed a massive success.

Conceptualizing the treats for that shop had been a fun challenge, just like every new international location had been.

She and Zack hadn't had a life since Roasted had really started to take off, nothing that went beyond coffee and confections, anyway. Of course, Zack was the backbone of the company, the man who got it done, the man who had seen it become a worldwide phenomenon.

They had drinks, coffee beans and mass-produced versions of her cupcakes and other goodies in all the major grocery chains in the U.S. Roasted was a household name. Because Zack was willing to sacrifice everything in his personal life to see it happen.

Hannah had been his only major concession to having a personal life, and that relationship had only started in the past year. And now Zack had lost her.

But he wasn't devastated. Apparently. She was probably more devastated than *he* was. Again, cake related.

"I didn't love her," he said.

Clara blinked. "You didn't…love her?"

"I cared about her. She was going to make a perfectly acceptable wife. But it wasn't like I was passionately head over heels for her or anything."

"Then why…why were you marrying her?"

"Because it was time for me to get married. I'm thirty. Roasted has achieved the level of success I was hoping for, and there comes a point where it's the logical step. I reached that point, Hannah had, too."

"Apparently she hadn't."

He gave her a hard glare. "Apparently."

"Do you know why? Have you talked to her?"

"She can come and talk to me when she's ready."

Zack would have laughed at the expression on Clara's face if he'd found anything remotely funny about the situation. The headlines would be unkind, and with so many media-hungry witnesses to the event, mostly on the absent bride's side, there would be plenty of people salivating to get their name in print by offering their version of the wedding of the century that wasn't.

Clara was too soft. Her brown eyes were all dewy looking, as though she were ready to cry on his behalf, her petite hands clasped in front of her, her shoulders slumped. She was more dressed up than he was used to seeing her. Her lush, and no he wasn't blind so of course he'd noticed, curves complemented, though not really displayed, by a dress that could only be characterized as nice, if a bit matronly.

She did that, dressed much older than she needed to, her thick auburn hair always pulled back into a low bun. Because she had to have her hair up to bake, and it had become a habit. But sometimes he wished she'd just let her hair down. And, because he was a man, sometimes he wished she wouldn't go to so much trouble to conceal her curves, either.

Although, in reality, her style of dress suited him. They worked together every day, and he had no business having an opinion on her physical appearance. His interest was purely for aesthetic purposes. Like opting for a room with a nice view.

That aside, Clara was all emotion and big hand gestures. There was nothing contained about her.

"I'm fine," he said.

"I know. I believe you," she said.

"No, you don't. Or you don't want to believe me because your more romantic sensibilities can't handle the fact that my heart isn't broken."

"Well, you ought to love the person you're going to marry, Zack."

"Why? Give me a good reason why. So that I could be more broken up about today? So that I could be more suitably wounded if she had shown up, and we had said our vows, when ten years on the marriage fell on the wrong side of the divorce statistics? I don't see the point in that."

"Well, I don't see the point at all."

"And I didn't ask."

"You never do."

"The secret to my success." His tone came out a bit harsher than he intended and Clara's expression reflected it. "You'll survive this," he said drily. "Breaking up is hard to do."

She rolled her eyes. "I'm worried about you."

"Don't be. I'm not so breakable. Tell me, any big word on the Japan location go up online while I was busy getting my photo taken?"

"All good. Some of the pictures I've been seeing are showing that it's absolutely slammed. And everything seems to be going over huge."

"Good. That means the likelihood of expanding further there is good." He sat down in one of the vacant, linen-covered chairs. They had pink bows. Also Hannah's choice. He put his hands on the tabletop, moving his mind away from the fiasco of a wedding day and getting it back on business. "How are things going with our designer cupcakes?"

"Um…well, I was pretty busy getting the wedding cake together." Clara felt like her head was spinning from the abrupt subject change.

Zack was in full business mode, sitting at the trussed up wedding-party table like it was the pared-down bamboo desk he had in his office at Roasted's corporate headquarters.

"And?"

"I have a few ideas. But these are pretty labor-intensive recipes and they really aren't practical for the retail line, or even for most of the stores."

"Cupcakes are labor intensive?"

She shot him a deadly look. "Why don't you try baking a simple batch and tell me how it goes?"

"No, thanks. I stick to my strengths, and none of them happen to involve baking."

"Then trust me, they're labor intensive."

"That's fine. My goal is to start doing a few boutique-style shops in some more affluent areas. We'll have bigger kitchens so that we'll have the capability to do more on-site baking."

"That could work. We'll have to have a more highly trained staff."

"That's fine. I'm talking about a few locations in Los Angeles, New York, Paris, London, that sort of thing. It will be more like the flagship store. A bit more personalized."

"I really like the idea, not that you'd care if I didn't."

"I am the boss."

"I know. I'm just the Vice President of Confections," she said, bringing up a joke they'd started in the early days of the company.

A smile touched his lips again and her heart expanded. "A big job."

"It is," she said. "And you don't pay me enough."

"Yes, I do."

She gave him a look. One she knew was less than scary, but she tried. "Anyway, go on."

"I had made an appointment to speak to a man who owns a large portion of farmland in Thailand. Small clusters of coffee and tea. All of his plants receive a very high level of care and that's making for extremely good quality roasts and brews. My goal is to set up a deal with him so we can get some limited-editions blends. We'll sell them in select locations, and have them available for order online."

Her mind skipped over all the details he'd just laid out, latching on to just one thing. "Weren't you going to Thailand on your honeymoon?"

"That was the plan."

Clara couldn't stop her mouth from dropping open. "You were going to do business on your honeymoon?"

"Hannah had some work to do, as well. Time doesn't stop just because you get married."

"No wonder she left you at the altar." She regretted the

words the moment they left her mouth. "Sorry. I didn't mean that."

"You did, and that's fine. Unlike you, Hannah had no romantic illusions, you can trust me on that. Her reasons for not showing up today may very well have had something to do with a Wall Street crisis. There's actually a good chance she's at her apartment, in her wedding gown, screaming obscenities at her computer screen watching the cost of grain go down."

She had to concede that the scenario was almost plausible. Hannah was all icy cool composure, and generally nice and polite, until someone crossed her in the corporate world. Clara had overheard the other woman's phone conversations become seriously cutthroat in tense business situations. Threats of removal of tender body parts had crossed her lips without hesitation.

She admired her for it. For the the intense way she went after what she wanted. She'd done it with Zack. It had been sort of awe inspiring to watch. Mostly it had been awe-inspiringly depressing. Because Clara wasn't cutthroat, or intense. And she hadn't been brave enough to pursue what she really wanted. She'd never been brave enough to pursue Zack.

"I doubt that's what happened," Clara said, even though she couldn't be certain.

"There was a reason I asked how the designer-cupcake thing was going."

"Oh." Back to business.

"I was trying to make sure you didn't feel swamped by the amount of work you have to do."

"No. Creating recipes is the best part of my job. I've been having fun with this one. I've actually done most of the experimental baking and tasting with our panel, and I have a few standout favorites, plus some that need to be improved. And then I'll have to narrow down the selection, because it just won't be feasible to have too many different kinds on the menu at once."

"So that was the long, detailed version of you telling me you aren't too busy at the moment?"

She shot him a deadly look. Jilted or not, he didn't need to be a jerk. "No, I'm not too busy."

"Good, because everything was set for me to head to Chiang Mai tonight."

"And you need me to make sure everything is running smoothly at corporate?" That wasn't usually the role she fulfilled. She wasn't an administrator, not even close.

"No, I want you to get packed, because you're coming with me."

Her stomach honestly felt like it plummeted, squeezing as it made its way down into her toes. "You're not serious. You're not actually asking me to come on your honeymoon with you?"

"The trip is booked. I have appointments made. I'm not canceling the honeymoon just because my bride neglected to show up." He looked at her, like he had thousands of times, but this time felt... It felt different. The inspection seemed closer somehow, his gray eyes more assessing, more intimate. She swallowed hard and tried to ignore the fact that her heart seemed to be trying to claw its way out of her chest. "I think you'll make a more than fitting replacement."

CHAPTER TWO

IF he had physically hit her he couldn't have possibly hurt her worse. A replacement? The consolation prize. The stand-in for tall, lean, angular Hannah who possessed the cheekbones of a goddess. Not that Clara had noticed, or compared.

Well, she had. And in some ways, on some days, the fact they were so different made it easier because there was no question of what the other woman had that she didn't.

But she had never, never put herself in the position of trying to vie for Zack's attention, not in that way. Because she'd known that she would be the consolation prize if he ever did decide to look in her direction. And she'd decided that was one thing she couldn't do to herself. The one thing worse than watching the man who meant the world to her tie himself to another woman. Being the one he'd settled for.

And now Zack was shoving her into that position. It made her want to gag.

"I'm not a replacement for anyone, Zack. And if you're suggesting I am, then I think we've become a little bit too comfortable with each other."

She turned and walked out of the reception hall. She left the cake. She didn't care about the cake. The staff of the hotel could have it for an early, sugary breakfast when they came in tomorrow morning.

She breezed through the hall and out the front doors, into

the damp, salty air. It had been a cool day, but now, with the sun dipping down below the horizon, the air coming in off of the bay was downright chilly. Which was good, because now, if anyone saw her lip tremble a little bit, she could blame the cold.

She didn't want to be emotional, not over something that wasn't even intentional, and with Zack, she knew it wasn't. Zack wasn't mean, more than that; he simply wasn't all that emotional, so he never assumed that anyone else was.

Everything was so surface to Zack. Nothing seemed to get under his skin. Nothing seemed to throw him off, even for a moment. Not even a canceled wedding.

Anyway, she'd had enough intentional digs taken at her in her life to know that things could get far too dramatic if she didn't make people have to work at hurting her feelings.

But since her feelings for Zack were a constant jumble, her reactions to anything involving him were always strong. Most of the time, though, she managed to keep that fact hidden from Zack. A lot of the time, she kept the extent of her feelings hidden from herself.

"Clara."

She turned and saw him standing just behind her. She didn't say anything. She crossed her arms beneath her breasts and fixed him with her best glare.

"You're the second woman to abandon me today."

Her face flooded with prickly heat. "See, that comparison is not very flattering, considering you've already used the word replacement in regards to me."

"That's not what I meant."

"Then what did you mean?"

"That I need someone to come with me, and actually, under the circumstances you're a better fit than my ex-fiancée."

For a full second she could only think of one thing his statement could possibly mean. Images clicked through her mind like close-up still-shots. Tan hands on a pale, bare hip.

Masculine lips on a feminine throat. Blood roared through her body, into her cheeks, making her face burn. She was sure they were the color of ripe strawberries, broadcasting her thoughts to anyone who looked at her.

"What?" she asked.

"Hannah's smart, don't get me wrong, but she doesn't know this market quite like you do. Prices on stocks, maybe, but it will be nice to have you on hand to offer an opinion about marketing and flavor."

Business. He was talking about business. And somehow, to Zack, business was more important than romance and making love on his honeymoon?

At least he was pretending it was. There was something different about his expression, a dark light behind his gray eyes. She'd seen Zack nearly every day for the past seven years. She knew his moods, his expressions as well as she knew her own.

And this was a different Zack. Well, she thought it was. For some reason, the hardness, the intensity, seemed more true than what she thought she knew of him.

Strange. But then, the whole day had been strange. Starting with the interminably long silence after the strains of the Bridal March had faded from the air and the aisle remained vacant.

All right, he'd made her mad. It wasn't the first time. He was bullheaded and a general pain in the butt sometimes. He was also the smartest man she knew, with a cutting wit that always kept her amused. He was one of the few people who'd never doubted that her ideas were good.

If she didn't go with him, she would spend her evenings hanging out by herself, reading and experimenting with cupcake recipes and licking the batter off the spatula. Fun, sure, but not the kind of fun she could have in Thailand.

Again, those images, erotic and explicit, assaulted her. No, that wasn't the kind of fun she would be having in Thailand.

Zack had never looked twice at her in that way and for the most part, she was fine with that. She'd had a crush on him at first, but even then she hadn't expected anything to come of it.

And, yes, Hannah had come in and stirred up some strange feelings. Because as long as Zack had simply been there, at work every day, and available for dinner meetings and a lot of other things, it had been comfortable. Zack was in every space in her life, at work and home.

But then along came Hannah, and she took up his time, and, Clara had assumed, that he loved her. And having to share Zack's emotion with someone else had felt... It had felt awful. And it had made her jealous, which didn't make sense because she'd never even tried to cross the boundaries of friendship with Zack. So it wasn't like Hannah had been encroaching on her territory or anything. But she'd been so jealous looking at Zack and Hannah she'd felt like her stomach was turning inside out, and she knew, that even if she could never have Zack, she didn't want anyone else to have him, either.

Which was just stupid and childish. About as stupid as going with a man on his honeymoon, platonically, in place of his bride, to conduct business with him. Platonically.

She needed her head checked. She needed some sanity. Maybe the problem was that Zack did take up all the spaces in her life. Maybe it would have to change.

Just the thought of that, of pushing him away, sent a sharp dose of pain through her system. She was addicted to him.

"All right. I'll go. Because I would rather have a paid vacation in Thailand than spend the week hanging out in the office and orchestrating the return of all your wedding presents."

"I'm not returning my wedding presents."

"You can't keep them, Zack."

"Of course I can. I might need a food processor someday. What does a food processor do?"

"I'll teach you sometime. Anyway, yes, I'll go with you."

The corner of his lip curved up into a wicked smile that

made her stomach tighten in a way that wasn't entirely unpleasant. "Excellent. Looks like I won't be spending my wedding night alone, after all."

It probably wasn't nice of him to tease Clara. But he liked the way her cheeks turned pink when he slipped an innuendo into the conversation. And frankly, he was in need of amusement after the day he'd had.

But amusement hadn't been his primary goal when he'd given her the wedding-night line out in front of the hotel. He'd been trying to atone for his ill-spoken remark about her being a replacement. In truth, he had more fun with Clara than he did with Hannah. It wasn't as though he disliked Hannah; quite the opposite. But he hadn't been marrying Hannah for the company.

She'd needed a husband to help her climb the corporate ladder, a little testosterone to help her out in a male-dominated field. And a wife...well, a wife like her was a convenience for a lot of reasons.

But Clara was not his wife. In a lot of ways, she was better. And he hadn't intended to hurt her feelings. She'd been quiet on the ride from the hotel back to her town house by the bay, and once they'd gotten inside to her place she'd dashed into her bedroom to pack a few things "real quick" which, in his experience with women meant...not quick at all.

He sat in her white leather chair, the one that faced her tiny television. Not state of the art at all, nothing like his place. The home theater had been one of his first major purchases when Roasted had become solvent. Clara's had been an industrial-grade mixer for her kitchen. That was where all *her* high-tech gear was. She had a stove with more settings than his stereo system.

"Ready." He looked up and his stomach clenched.

Clara was standing at the end of the hallway, large, pink leather bag draped over her shoulder, dark jeans conforming to the curve of her hips, and a black knit top outlining the contours of her very generous breasts. He hadn't gotten married today, so he was going to allow himself a longer look than he ever did. He'd noticed her body before, but he'd never allowed himself to really look at her as a man looked at a woman. He didn't know why he was letting himself do it now. A treat in exchange for the day, maybe. Or exhaustion making him sloppy with his rules.

Clara was an employee. Clara was a friend. Clara was not a possible lover, and normally that meant no looking at her like she could be.

But tonight wasn't normal. Not by a long stretch.

"Good." He stood up and tried to keep his interest in her body sublimated. But he was just a man. A man who had been celibate for a very long time. A man who had been expecting a reprieve on that and had been sadly disappointed.

"Are we taking the company jet?" She smiled, her perfectly shaped brow raised.

She really was beautiful, and not just her curves. He didn't stop to notice her looks very often. She was like...not furniture, but a fixture for sure. Someone who was always there, every day, no matter what. And when someone was always there, you didn't stop and look at them very often.

But he was looking at her now. Her face was a little bit round, her skin pale and soft. Her eyes, dark brown and wide, were fringed with dark lashes, surprising given her auburn hair color. And her lips...full and soft looking, a very delicate shade of pink.

Looking at her features was a nice distraction, especially since he was about to make her very, very angry. Normally he didn't care for other people's feelings. Not enough to lose any sleep over. He was in command of his world, and he didn't question his decisions.

But Clara was different. She'd always been different.

"There's something I didn't tell you yet." And it might have been wise to save it until she was safely on the plane. And had had a glass or two of champagne.

"What's that?" she asked, eyes narrowing.

"I was supposed to get married today."

Her eyes became glittering, deadly slits. "Right."

"I was meant to be going on my honeymoon with my wife. And now, here I find myself jilted. No bride. Barely any pride to speak of."

She arched her brow, her mouth twisted into a sour expression. "What, Zack?"

"I need you to come with me. As more than my friend. Not really more than my friend, but more as far as Amudee is concerned."

She shook her head and let her pink bag slip off of her shoulder and onto the hardwood floor. "That's...that's insane! Who would believe you'd hooked up with someone else already?"

"Everyone, Clara. I'm a man who, as far as the public is concerned, is in the throes of heartbreak. Everyone knows about our business relationship. About our friendship. Is it so insane to think that, after suffering heartbreak, I looked to my closest friend and found so much more?"

Oh, it was sick. It really was. To hear him saying something that was...that was so close to her real-life fantasies it was painful to listen to the words fall from his lips. "No. No, I am not playing this game. That's ridiculous, Zack. Go on your own."

"I can't."

"Why?"

"Look, my pride will survive. But if I show up alone, and without my wife, looking the part of lonely loser who couldn't hold on to his woman...well, who wants to cut a business deal with that guy?"

"So offer him more money," she hissed.

"That's the thing with Amudee. Money isn't the main objective. If I could throw a bigger check at him, I would. But it's not only about that. It's about people, the kind of people he wants to do business with, and for the most part, I am that man. I care deeply about fair trade, about the work he has going on there in Thailand. I have to look like I call the shots in my own life, and I will not let an inconsequential hiccup like Hannah's cold feet affect that."

She shook her head. "No. Zack just…"

"If I lose the deal because of this…"

"I'm fired? I doubt it. And I can't imagine him passing this up just because you aren't getting married now."

"This growing project is a huge thing for him, his life's work. He's poured his entire fortune into this. He has high principles, and, yes, a lot of it does have to do with bringing money into Northern Thailand, for the people that live there, but he won't go into something if he doesn't feel one hundred percent about it. I can't afford to let it slip to ninety-nine percent. And if you tip the deal over, then I need you."

"So buy your beans from someone else," she said. "Someone who doesn't care what your personal life looks like."

"There is no one else. Not with a product like this. He understands the foundation I've built Roasted on. That it's always been my goal to find small, family run farms to support. He's a philanthropist and what he's done is give different families in the north of Thailand their own plots to cultivate their own crops. Tea and coffee is being grown there, of the highest quality. And I want the best—I don't want to settle for second."

Clara bent and picked her bag up from the floor. She really hated what Zack was proposing. Not just because she didn't exactly relish the idea of lying to someone for a week; there was that, but also because the idea of playing the part of his lover for a week made her feel sick.

She'd done a good job, a damn good job, of pretending that all she felt for Zack was friendship, with a very successful working relationship thrown into the mix. She'd pretended, not just for him, but for herself.

Because she didn't want to desire a man who was so out

of her league. A man who dated women who were her polar opposites in looks and personality. Women who were tall and thin, blonde and as cool and in control at all times as he was.

Wanting Zack was a pipe dream of the highest order.

Yes, it had been harder to ignore those sneaky, forbidden feelings when his engagement was announced, but she'd still done it. She'd baked his wedding cake, for heaven's sake.

But this, this was one ask too many. Even for him. To go to a romantic setting, pretend she was experiencing her deepest fantasy, all for show, just seemed too masochistic.

And yet, it was hard to say no to him, too. Not when, as much as it galled to be asked to do this, it would give her this sort of strange, out of time, experience with him.

And definitely not when the whole thing was such a big deal to the future of Roasted. Her wagon was well and truly hitched to the company, and in order for her to succeed, the company had to succeed.

Her wagon was hitched to more than the company, if she was honest. It was Zack. Zack and his wicked smiles, Zack and that indefinable thing he possessed that made her want to care for him, even though he never let her.

Zack was the reason she didn't date. Not because, as a boss he kept her so busy with work, though she'd pretended that was it for a long, long time. It was Zack the man. Because her feelings for him were more than just complicated. And she was... she was a doormat.

She'd baked the man's wedding cake. And then what had she thought would happen? She was going to stay at Roasted, after Zack married? Play Aunt Clara to his kids? Watch while he had this whole life while she died a virgin with nothing but her convection oven for company?

Sick. It was sick.

And now she was really going with him to Chiang Mai to play the part she knew he'd never really consider her for?

She needed to get a life.

She was right. What she'd thought earlier at the hotel had been right. A moment of clarity. It wasn't healthy to have him in everything. He was her boss, her best friend. He filled her work and personal hours, and even when he wasn't around, he was in her thoughts. Zack had dates, he had a life that didn't include her and she...didn't. She couldn't do it anymore.

"If I do this... If I do this, then it's going to be the last thing I do at Roasted." She thought about the bakery, the one she'd been dreaming of for the past few months. The one she'd drawn up plans for. It had been in her mind ever since Zack and Hannah got engaged. Just a mere fantasy of escaping that painful reality at first, but now...now she thought she needed to make it happen.

She needed to make some boundaries. Have something that was hers. Just hers.

"What?" he asked, his dark brows locking together.

"If I go with you and play arm candy then I'm done. It's not...it's not the first time I've thought of this." It wasn't. When he'd come into the office with Hannah and announced that the whole thing was official, well, she'd just about handed in her resignation then and there.

But of course his smile and his innate Zack-ness had stopped her. Because in her mind, it was better to have crumbs from him than everything from someone else. Because he was so enmeshed in her life, so a part of her routine. Her first thought in the morning, her constant companion throughout the day. And it was his face she saw when she drifted off to sleep.

He was everything.

And the real truth of the situation was that while Zack cared for her, and even loved her, possibly like some sort of younger sister figure, she wasn't everything to him. And he didn't want her the way she wanted him.

"What the hell?" he asked.

"I'm...I'm having a revelation, hold on."

"Could you not?"

"No. I'm sorry. I'm…I'm sorry, Zack. This really has been… It's been brewing for a while and I know it wasn't the best day or the best way to say it, but…it does have to be said."

"Why?"

"Because… Because it's eating my life!" The words exploded from her. "And if that isn't made completely obvious by the fact that I'm agreeing to drop everything at the spur-of-the-moment to fly to Asia to go on your honeymoon in place of your fiancée and pretend to be your *new* girlfriend…well…I can't help you."

"No. No, I don't agree."

"And what, Zack? You can't force me to stay at my job."

He looked like he was searching for some loophole that would in fact give him that authority.

"I need a good severance, too. I want to open my own bakery."

"The hell you will!" he said, his voice hard, harsher than she'd ever heard.

"The hell I won't," she returned, keeping her own voice steady, though, how she managed, she wasn't sure.

"Non-compete."

"What?"

"You signed a non-compete."

"A bakery would not compete with Roasted, not really," she said, planting her hands on her hips.

"It could, on a technicality, especially as we'd likely share a very similar desserts menu, seeing as you planned all of mine."

"I'm not talking about a worldwide bakery chain, I'm talking… I want to open one up that I run myself. Here in San Francisco. Something personal, something me. Something that would give me a chance to have a life."

"No."

It was shocking, Zack's transformation from unaffected, jilted groom, to this. She would have expected this kind of reaction from Hannah not showing up to the wedding, not to her asking to quit the business. Where was his control? Zack always had control. Always.

Except now.

"Then I won't go with you. And I get the feeling that a female companion is a bit more important than you let on. I know you too well for you to hide it from me."

His gray eyes glittered in the dim light of her apartment. "There is some competition. Sand Dollar Coffee is competing for the chance to get these same roasts, and Mr. Amudee, traditionalist he is, is very likely to give preference to their CEO. They were just there for a week in the villa, Martin Cole, his wife and their four children. Mr. Amudee was charmed."

"So you do need me. You need me to give you an edge. To make sure Amudee knows you're a macho man who can have his way with whomever, whenever. We're friends, Zack. I don't know why it has to be like this...."

"You were the one leveraging," he bit out.

"Because I can't do this anymore. The beck-and-call thing. I need more. *You* were getting married, you should get that."

"You want to get married?"

Her stomach tightened. "Not necessarily. But I don't even have a hope of it as long as I'm working sixty-hour weeks. And since I don't believe in practical arrangements, like the one you and Hannah have, that will keep me from having a successful relationship."

"Fine," he said, the word stiff. "But you stay on until the deal with Amudee is done. Got it? I'll need you to be around, at the business, my assumed lover, until the ink is dry on the contract."

It was cold and mercenary. And it was tempting. Tempting to play the part. To immerse herself in it for a while. Just thinking about it made her stomach tighten, made her shiver.

No. You can't forget. This is just a game to him. More business. "Yes. I won't let you down. If I say I'm going to do something, I'll do it."

"I know."

"And when it's over?"

"You can open your bakery. I'll make sure you're compensated for your time here."

Clara stuck out her hand, her heart cracking in her chest. "Then I think we have a deal."

CHAPTER THREE

ZACK was in a fouler mood than he'd been when the double doors of the hotel's wedding hall had opened to reveal, not his bride, but a very panicked wedding coordinator who was hissing into her headset.

He leaned back in his seat on his private plane and stared at the amber liquid in the tumbler on his tray. Turbulence was bouncing the alcohol around, sending the strong aroma into the air. He wasn't tempted to take a drink. He didn't drink, it was just that his flight attendant had heard about the disaster and assumed he might be in need.

He looked across the wide aisle at Clara, who was, sitting on a leather love seat in the living-room-style plane cabin, staring fixedly at her touch-screen phone.

"Good book?" he asked.

Her head snapped up. "How did you know I was reading?"

"Because you always read."

"Books make better company than surly bosses."

"Do they make better company than bitchy employees? If so, perhaps I should read more."

She looked at him, her expression bland. "I wouldn't know."

"No. You wouldn't. Look, I gave you what you asked for."

"After a big ugly fight."

"Because I don't want to lose you."

A strange expression flashed in her brown eyes. "Right."

"You've been here since the very early days of Roasted, and you've been key to the success of the company, of course I don't want to lose you."

She looked back down at her phone. "Well, I can't live my entire life to make you happy."

He frowned. "That's not how it's been, is it?"

"No," she said, her tone grudging. She put her phone down and stretched her legs out in front of her and her arms straight over her head, back arching, thrusting her breasts forward. His body hardened, his blood rushing through his veins hotter and faster.

That was a direct result of the fact that he was supposed to break his long bout with celibacy tonight, on this very plane, and it wasn't happening now. Still, his body hadn't caught up with his mind yet. Damned inconvenient considering he was now fixating on his friend's breasts. Breasts that he was not supposed to fixate on. Basically two of the only breasts on earth that were off-limits to him.

More inconvenient, considering they were about to spend the week in Chiang Mai in a very secluded and gorgeous honeymoon villa. Even more when you considered that she was leaving the company soon after.

Well, that wasn't happening. He would make sure of that. He would offer her whatever he had to offer to get her to stay, and until then he would simply nod whenever she brought it up.

He wasn't sure how he would convince her, only that he would. He'd successfully stolen her away from her bakery job back when he'd only had a handful of coffee shops to his name. He had no doubt he could do an even better job of keeping her now that he had so many resources at his disposal. He could give her whatever she wanted, more freedom, more time off. And she was his friend. She wouldn't leave him.

She was just mad about the whole fake fiancée thing. But she would get over it. She always did. It wasn't the first time he'd made her mad. Likely it wouldn't be the last. But that was just how it was. She wouldn't really leave him.

He was a master negotiator. And he didn't lose. He was good at keeping control, of his life and of his business.

"The property we're staying on is supposed to be amazing. It borders a Chiang Mai, and there's a spa right on site. It's more of a resort than anything else, but you have to be invited to stay there by the owner. Very exclusive." He got nothing but silence in response.

"They have unicorns, I hear," he continued, "with golden hooves. You'll love it."

He heard her try to stifle a very reluctant snicker.

He leaned in and looked at her face, at the faint shadows marring the pale skin beneath her eyes. "Are you tired?" he asked.

She leaned back in the chair. "You have no idea."

"There's a bedroom." His blood jumped in his veins again, like the kick-start on a motorcycle. "You could lay down for a while if you want."

"How long have we got?"

"Ten more hours."

"Oh, yeah, I need sleep." She stood up and did another little stretch move that accentuated her breasts.

Clara needed more than sleep. She needed to get out of the tiny, enclosed space with Zack and all of his hot, male phero-mones that were wreaking havoc on her good sense. If she had any at all to wreak havoc on. Well, she did have some. She'd used it to ask for her out.

For a little bit of a chance to move on and forward with her life. Because Zack hadn't married Hannah today, which was fine and good, but he would marry someone. He'd decided to, and when Zack put his mind to something, he did it. That meant it would happen, sometime in the very near future, she imag-ined, now that she knew love wasn't necessarily on the docket. Heck, if he smiled just right at the flight attendant they would probably be engaged by the time they landed in Thailand. And then she could sleep in the guest room in the villa.

She snorted.

"What?" he asked.

"Nothing."

"The scariest word known to man when issued from the lips of a woman."

Her lip curled voluntarily at his statement. "Sexist."

"I prefer realist, but you're free to call it as you see it."

"So tell me this, Zack."

"What?" he asked, one dark eyebrow arched.

"I assume you'll attempt marriage again."

"If I find the right woman."

"And by that, you don't mean the woman you love?"

Something in Zack's posture changed, subtle but obvious to her, his shoulders straightening, his muscles tensing beneath his expertly tailored shirt. His eyes changed, too. There was something dark there, haunted, something she'd never seen before, not this clearly. She'd felt it before, an intensity lurking beneath his cool exterior, but she'd never seen it so plainly.

It was almost frightening in its intensity, transforming a man she'd seen every day for seven years into a cold stranger.

"I don't do love, Clara. Ever." He turned his focus to the newspaper that was folded on his lap. "Good night."

Clara turned toward the bedroom, exhaustion burrowing beneath her skin, down into her bones. Yesterday, everything had been the way it had always been. It had sucked; it had been heading in a direction she hadn't liked, but for the most part, it had been the same.

Today everything felt different. Most of it was her fault. And even though she wouldn't change it, she hated it.

"We just landed."

Clara sat up and pushed the wild mass of auburn curls out of her eyes. She blinked a few times and Zack's face came into focus. For a moment, she didn't do anything. She didn't move, she didn't breathe, she just concentrated on his face being the first thing she saw.

She'd never woken up next to a man before. And, yeah, this wasn't really waking up next to a man in the traditional sense. And he was more leaning over than next to her. But it was a really nice thought, and it was a very nice sight first thing in the morning. If it was even morning. She had no idea.

"What time is it?" she asked.

"It's 10:00 p.m. local time."

She flopped backward. "Oh, no. Why did you let me sleep?"

"I tried to wake you."

"No, you didn't."

"I did, you were out."

She felt a strange sort of disappointment curling in her stomach. She wished, well, part of her did, that he had woken her up. She swallowed hard. Her throat felt like it was lined with cotton. It was far too easy to think of a lot of very interesting ways he might have woken her up.

No. Bad.

"I'm going to be a wreck."

"Sorry."

"I take it you didn't sleep?" She looked down and realized she was still wearing her jeans.

"No. But then, I don't sleep all that much."

That didn't surprise her. She'd never really quizzed him on his sleeping habits, but honestly, he just didn't seem like the kind of man who could sleep at all. He had too much energy and drive to stop even for a moment. Whenever she'd thought of him in bed...well, it hadn't been images of him sleeping plaguing her.

"We're at the airport?" she asked, peering out one of the windows, confused by how dark it was outside.

"Don't know if I'd say airport so much as landing strip.

We're on Mr. Amudee's property. It backs the city, but there's a lot of forest in between his land and civilization."

"Oh."

"There's a car waiting for us, and your luggage, such as it was, is already loaded in it."

She stood and her breasts nearly brushed his chest. She'd misjudged the distance. Her breath caught in her throat and nearly choked her.

Zack didn't seem affected at all. He just smiled at her, one of his wicked smiles, all of the ghosts she'd glimpsed in his gray eyes before she'd gone to sleep were banished now, leaving behind nothing but the glint that was so familiar to her.

"I didn't have—" she had to take in another breath because being so close to him had kind of sucked the other one out of her "—that much time to pack. Otherwise I could have had just as many bags as your high-maintenance ladies."

"You aren't like the women I date. You aren't high maintenance. I like that about you." He turned and headed out the bedroom and she followed him, her chest suddenly feeling tight.

What he meant was, she wasn't beautiful. Not like the women he dated. The women who were all high-fashion planes and angles. And cheekbones.

Her mother was like that. Her sister, too. Tall and leggy with hip bones that were more prominent than their breasts. And that was the look that walked runways. The look that was fashionable, especially in southern California.

And she just didn't have the look. She had curves. An abundance of them. If any of the chi-chi boutiques had bras with her cup size, they were very often too small around, meant for women who'd gone under the knife to give them what nature had bestowed upon her so liberally. And her stomach was a little bit round, not concave or rippling. She wasn't sure if she'd ever seen her ribs.

Standing next to the women in her family just made her

feel…inadequate. And wide. And short. She'd tried to subsist on cabbage and water like her mother and sister, but frankly, she'd felt like garbage and had decided a long time ago that feeling healthy beat being fifteen pounds lighter.

Of course, that decision didn't erase a lifetime of insecurity. And that insecurity wasn't all down to weight, either.

"Great. Glad to be so…easy."

The door to the plane was standing open, and a staircase had been lowered to the tarmac. Zack stood and waited for her to go in front of him. She passed him without looking, trying not to show the knockout effect the slight scent of his cologne had on her as she moved by him.

"I wouldn't call you easy," he said.

She stopped, third stair from the top, and whipped around to look at him. "That's not what I meant."

"Not what I meant, either," he said, his expression overly innocent.

"Yeah. Right. Are you determined to drive me absolutely insane for this whole trip?" She continued down the steps and hopped onto the tarmac, the night air balmy and thick with mist, blowing across her cheeks and leaving its moist hand-print behind.

"We are supposed to be a couple."

"Fair enough."

She was reluctant to get into the glossy black town car that was parked right by the plane. Because she'd only just gotten Zack-free air, and she didn't really relish the thought of getting right back into a tight, enclosed space with him.

She needed to be able to breathe. To think. And she couldn't do it when he was around.

That realization alone reinforced her crazy, spur-of-the-moment decision to move on with her life, and away from Roasted.

The idea made her slightly sick and more than a little bit sad. Roasted had been her life since Zack had hired her on. The day-to-day of it, the constant push to invent more and more goodies, to push the flavor profiles, to push her creativity... there would never be anything else like it.

But she needed to stand on her own feet. To move on with life. She'd gone from her parents to Zack, and while she didn't feel familial about Zack in any way, he represented comfort and safety. And other stuff that wasn't comforting or safe. But being with him, like she was, wasn't pushing her to move forward.

So she was pushing herself. It was uncomfortable, but that was the way it worked. She hoped it would work.

He opened the door to the town car for her and she slid inside, and he came in just behind her. "So, do you and your boyfriends have fights?"

He must know she never had boyfriends. The odd disastrous date that never went past the front door. Emphasis on the odd, since half the men picked her up while she happened to be in the flagship store. And, in her experience, men who picked you up at ten in the morning in coffeehouses were a bit strange.

"How many long-term relationships have I had, Zack?"

"Well, Pete was around a lot until he moved for work."

"Pete? He was a friend from high school. And I was not his type, if you catch my drift."

"You weren't blonde?"

"Or male."

"Oh."

"Point being, I haven't done a lot of long-term." Any, but whatever. "And if I'm ever going to...move on, go into that phase of life then I need to be less consumed with work."

A muscled in his jaw ticked. "But you won't make this kind of money running your own bakery."

"I know. But I have a decent amount of money. How much do I need? How much do you need?"

There was a pause. Zack's hand curled into a fist on the leather seat, then relaxed. "More. Just...a bit more."

"And then you're never done."

"But if not for that then what am I working for?"

She swallowed. "A good question. Good and scary. Though I suppose adding a wife will add…something. When you find a new prospect, that is. Did Hannah have an equally efficient and driven sister, by chance?"

"Not that I'm aware of."

She snapped her fingers. "Darn."

"Don't lose sleep over it."

"I won't be sleeping tonight, anyway. Because you didn't wake me up on the plane." She couldn't resist the jab.

"Because you sleep like a rock and snore like a walrus."

"Might be why my relationships aren't long-term," she said drily. Not that any man had ever heard her snore but she was so not admitting to that.

"I doubt that."

"Do you?"

His eyes locked with hers and something changed in the air. It seemed to crackle. Like a spark on dry leaves. It was strange. It was breathtaking, and electrifying, and she never wanted it to end.

"Why?" she asked, pressing. Desperate to hear more. A little bit afraid of hearing more, too.

"Because a little bit of snoring wouldn't deter a man who'd had the pleasure of sharing your bed."

She sucked in a sharp breath and looked out the window, and into the inky-black jungle. She felt dizzy. She felt…hot.

"Well, thanks," she said.

He chuckled, low and rich like the best chocolate ganache. Just as bad for her to indulge in as the naughty treat, too. "You seem uncomfortable with the compliment."

"You and I don't talk about things like that."

"Only because it hadn't come up."

"Do you snore?" she asked.

"Not that I'm aware of."

"Then your lack of long-term relationships doesn't really make sense at all."

He arched one dark brow. "Was that a compliment?"

"More a commentary on the transient nature of your love life."

"I'm wounded."

She winced. "Well, maybe in light of all that happened today it wasn't the best thing to say."

"You've never pulled punches before, don't start now."

"I don't know any other way to be."

"Now that may account for your own short-term relationships."

She whipped around to face him and her heart stalled. He was looking at her like she was a particularly interesting treat. One he might like to taste.

The car stopped and she nearly breathed a prayer of thanks out loud. She needed distance. She needed it desperately.

"Well," Zack said, opening the door. "Time to go and have a look at our honeymoon suite."

CHAPTER FOUR

THE honeymoon villa was the epitome of romance. The anterior wall of the courtyard was surrounded by dense, green trees, clinging vines and flowers covering most of the stone wall, adding color, a sense that nature ruled here, not man. There was a keypad on the gate and Zack entered a code in; a reminder that the man very much had his fingerprints all over the property.

"Nice," she said, as the gates swung open and revealed an open courtyard area. The villa itself was white and clean. Intricate spires, carved from wood and capped in gold, adorned the roof of the house, rising up to meet the thick canopy of teak trees.

"Mr. Amudee had planned on giving Hannah and I a few days of wedded bliss prior to meeting with me, so he made sure I had the code, and that everything in the home would be stocked and ready."

Clara tried not to think about Zack and Hannah, using the love nest for its intended purpose. More than that, she tried not to think of her and Zack using it for its intended purpose.

She really did try. There was no point in allowing those fantasies. Those fantasies had led to nothing more than dateless Friday nights and lack of sleep.

"Well, that was…thoughtful of him."

"It was. I believe he has some activities planned for us, too."

Oh, great. She was going to be trapped in happy-couple-honeymoon-activity hell.

She followed Zack through the vast courtyard and to the wide, ornately carved double doors at the front of the villa. She touched one of the flower blossoms etched into the hard surface. "These are gorgeous. I wonder if I could mimic the design with frosting."

"I will happily be a part of that experiment." He pushed open the doors and stood, waiting for her to go in before him.

"You do seem to hang around a lot more when I'm practicing my baking skills."

"I don't know how."

"I could teach you," she said. "Maybe sometimes after I can teach you how to use a food processor."

"I think I'll pass. Anyway, I'm a bachelor. Have pity on me. I wasn't supposed to be a bachelor after today, but I am, and now I still need my best friend to cook for me."

"And probably do your laundry."

"I wouldn't mind."

Basically he wanted her to be his wife with none of the perks. She nearly said so, but that would sound too much like she wanted the perks, and even if a part of her did, she'd rather parade naked through the Castro District than confess it.

"I'm not doing your laundry."

Zack closed the door behind them and a shock of awareness hit her, low and strong in her stomach. She felt so very alone with Zack all of a sudden that she could hardly breathe. And it wasn't as though she'd never been alone with him. She had been. Hundreds of times. Late nights in the office, at her apartment cooking, at his luxury penthouse watching a movie.

But this wasn't San Francisco. It wasn't their offices; it wasn't one of their apartments. It felt like another world entirely and that was…dangerous.

She looked up at the tall, peaked ceilings, at the intricately carved vines and flowers that cascaded from wooden rafters.

Swaths of fabric were the only dividers between rooms, gauzy and sexy, providing the illusion of privacy without actually giving any at all.

And in the middle of it all was Zack. He filled the space, not just with his breadth and height, but with his presence. With the unique scent that was so utterly Zack mingling with the heavy perfume of plumeria. Familiar and exotic all at once.

This was like one of her late-night fantasies. Like a scene she'd only ever allowed herself to indulge in when she was shrouded in the darkness of her room. And now, those fantasies were coming back to bite her.

Because they were mingling with reality. This was real. And in reality, Zack didn't want her like she wanted him. But in her fantasies he did. There, he touched her like a lover, his eyes locked with hers, his lips…

She needed her head checked.

"I have a housekeeper, anyway. I was teasing," he said.

"I know." She hoped she didn't look as flushed as she felt.

"I don't think you did. I think you were about to bite my head off." He looked…amused. Damn him.

"Is there food?"

His lips curved into a half smile. "I can check."

He wandered out of the main living area, in search of the kitchen, she imagined, and she took the opportunity to breathe in air that didn't smell of Zack. Air that didn't make her stomach twist.

She walked the opposite direction of Zack, through one of the fabric-covered doorways and stopped. It was the bedroom. The bed was up on a raised platform, a duvet in deep red spread over it. Cream colored fabric with delicate gold vines woven throughout hung from the ceiling, shielding the bed. It was obvious that it wasn't a bed made for one, or for sleeping.

She swallowed heavily, her eyes glued to the center of the room.

She heard footsteps behind her and turned. "I found food."

"Good," she said, trying to ignore the fast-paced beating of her heart. Zack and the bed in one room was enough to make her feel like her head might explode. "There is... I mean, this isn't the only bedroom is it?"

"I'm not sure."

"Oh," she said.

"I set dinner out on the balcony, if you want to join me."

"Don't you want to go to bed?" she asked, then immediately regretted the way the words had come out. Heat flooded her face, and she was certain there was a very blatant blush staining her cheeks. "I mean...well, you know what I mean. That wasn't... I meant you. By yourself. Because I slept and I know you didn't."

"At least let me buy you dinner first, Clara," he said, his mouth curved in amusement, his eyes glittering with the same heat she'd noticed earlier. It made her uncomfortable. And jittery. And a little bit excited.

She laughed, a kind of nervous, fake sound. "Of course."

Zack ignored the jolt of arousal that shot through his veins. For a moment at least, he and Clara had both been thinking the same thing. And it had involved that bed. That bed that was far too tempting, even for a man who prided himself on having absolute control at all times.

Things with Clara had always been easy. No, he'd never been blind to her beauty, but their relationship had never been marked by moments of heavy sexual tension. Not until today.

And knowing that, even for a moment, she'd shared in the temptation, well, that made it all worse. Or better. No, definitely worse, because in his life, he valued boundaries. Everything and everyone had a place and a purpose. Clara had a place. It was not in his bed.

Or this bed.

It was important that his life stay focused like that. Controlled. That nothing crossed over. He'd been rigid in that, uncompromising, for the past fourteen years.

"This way, beautiful," he said, clenching his hand into a fist to keep from putting it on Clara's lower back. He would have done it before. But suddenly it seemed like far too risky of a maneuver.

Clara shot him a look that was pure Clara, his friend, and it made the knot in his chest ease slightly. Though it didn't do much for the heat coursing through his veins.

He was questioning why he'd thought bringing her was a good idea. And he never questioned his decisions. Not anymore. Because he thought everything through before he acted. Not thinking, letting anything go before reason, was a recipe for disaster.

And bringing Clara had been the logical choice. At least until thirty seconds ago.

He moved in front of her, under the guise of leading her to the deck, but really just so he wouldn't let himself look at her butt while she walked. Occasionally he allowed himself the indulgence of looking at her curves. Harmless enough. He was human, a man, and she was a beautiful woman. But it seemed less harmless after a moment like that.

"This is really nice," she said when they were outside.

Her words were true, banal and safe. He'd set the table and turned on the string of lanterns that were hung above the table. A moderate effort, but he had wanted it to be nice. Now it felt strangely intimate.

He couldn't remember the last time a dinner date had seemed intimate. He couldn't even remember the last time that word had seemed applicable to something in his life. Very often, sex didn't even seem all that intimate to him.

Of course, it had been so long since he'd had sex maybe that wasn't true. That was likely half of his problem now.

Clara wandered to the railing and leaned over the edge, tossing her glossy copper curls over her shoulder and sniffing the air. Or maybe the sex wasn't the problem. Because being alone with Hannah hadn't made him feel this way. And there were days when the scent of Clara's perfume hitting him when she walked past made his stomach tighten...

But he ignored that. He was good at ignoring it.

"What are you doing?"

"It smells amazing out here. Like when you bake bread and the air is heavy with it. Only it's flowers instead of flour." She turned to him and smiled, the familiar glitter back in her eyes.

The knot inside him eased even more.

"I would never have thought of it that way." He pulled her chair out and nodded toward it and she walked over to the table and took her seat.

He sat across from her, ladling reheated *Tom Yum Ka* into her bowl and then into his. She smiled at him, the slight dimple in her rounded cheeks deepening as she did.

Things seemed to have stabilized, even if her sweet grin did have an impact on his stomach.

"So, tell me more about this deal with Mr. Amudee."

He put his forearm on the table and leaned forward. "I think we covered most of it. Although, another reason it's nice to have you here is your palate. I'd like you to taste the different roasts and come up with pairings for them. It would be particularly nice to have in our boutique locations."

"Pairings!" Her eyes glittered. "I love it."

"Good coffee or tea really is just as complex as good wine. There are just as many flavor variations."

"I know, Zack," she said.

"Of course you do. You appreciate good coffee. It's one reason we get along so well."

Clara took another bite of her soup and let the ginger sit on her tongue, enjoying the zip of spice that hurt just enough to take her mind off the weird reaction she was having to Zack. Yes, being attracted to him was nothing new.

But this was different. The attraction she felt at home was like a sleeper agent. It attacked her when she least expected it. In dreams. When she was looking at other men and contemplating accepting a date. It wasn't usually this shaky, limb-weakening thing that made her feel tongue-tied and exposed in his presence. Maybe it was the feeling of utter seclusion. Or maybe it was because she knew just what that big bed was here for, what he'd been planning on doing with it.

"That and I bake you cupcakes," she said, swallowing the tart and spicy soup.

"There is that." Zack looked toward the railing of the deck, off into trees, the look in his eyes distant, cold suddenly. "Tell me about your bakery."

"The one I hope to have?"

"Yes. And the life you're going to put with it."

Her chest constricted. "It will be small. I'll have regular menu items and daily specials. I'll have more time to make fancy little treats with a lot of decorations. I'll have a hand in everything instead of just conceptualizing and farming the instructions out to hordes of employees."

"And that's important to you?"

"It's how we started. Me in the flagship store, you going back and forth between your— What did you have when I met you? Fifteen stores up and down the West Coast? It was fun."

"Yes, but now we have money."

She nodded. "We do. And it's great. You've done this incredible thing, Zack. The growth has been…amazing. Way beyond what I imagined."

"Not beyond what I imagined."

"No?"

He shook his head. "It was always the plan. Planning is key. It's when you don't plan, when you drift, that's when things are a surprise. Good or bad."

"You didn't plan for Hannah to opt out of the wedding."

"I didn't plan for you to leave Roasted, either. Sometimes other people come in and mess with your plans," he said, his dark eyebrows locked together.

"This doesn't mean I won't see you anymore," she said.

Though she probably shouldn't. But the thought of that made her chest feel like there was a hole in it. Still, she'd baked the man's wedding cake. She was such a pushover, such a hopeless case, it was obscene. It had to end.

She didn't want it to. But if she didn't see him at work every day…it would be a start.

"I know you'll still see me," he said, his mouth curving. "You'd have withdrawals otherwise."

If only that weren't true. "Right. Can't live without you, Zack." She felt her throat get tight. *Stupid.* So stupid. But Zack really did mean the world to her, and she had a very strong suspicion that her statement was nothing but the truth. He had offered her support when no one else in her life had. He still did.

She regretted saying she wanted to leave Roasted. Regretted it with everything in her. But she couldn't change her mind. The reasoning behind the decision was still sound. And she really would still see him. He just wouldn't fill up her whole world anymore. She couldn't let feelings for him, feelings that would never be returned, hold her back for the rest of her life.

Zack's arm twitched and he reached into his pocket. "Phone vibrated," he said. He pulled out his smart phone and unlocked the screen, a strange expression on his face. "Hannah texted me."

"Really?"

"She's really sorry about the wedding."

"Oh, good," Clara snorted. The weird jealousy and protectiveness were back together again. She was still righteously angry at Hannah for what she'd done, even while she was relieved.

"She met someone else."

"What?"

"Yes." He looked up, his expression neutral. "She's in love apparently."

"And she's texting this to you?"

He shrugged. "It fits our relationship."

"No, it doesn't. Love or not, you still had a relationship."

"We weren't sleeping together."

Clara felt her stomach free fall down into her toes. "What?" That didn't even make sense. Hannah was a goddess. A sex bomb that had been detonated in the middle of her life, making her feel inadequate and inexperienced.

And he hadn't slept with her? She'd assumed—imagined even, in sadly graphic detail—that half of the meetings in his office had been rousing desk-sex sessions. And...they hadn't been? So much angst. So much stomach curling angst exerted over...nothing, it turned out.

"Why?" she asked, her voice several notches higher than usual.

"Hannah's kind of traditional. Because we weren't in love... well, she needed love or marriage. We were going to have marriage."

"Hmm. Well, then maybe texting is appropriate. I don't understand how you were going to marry this woman."

"Marriage is a business agreement, like anything else, Clara. You decide if you can fulfill the obligations and if they'll be advantageous to you. Then you sign or you don't."

"Cynical."

"True."

"Then why bother to get married? I don't understand."

He shrugged. "Because it's the thing to do. Marriage offers stability, companionship. It's logical."

"Good grief, Spock. Logical. That's not why people get married." She snorted again. "Did your parents have a horrible divorce or something?"

Zack shook his head. "No."

"You never talk about your family."

He looked down at his soup. "Not on accident."

"Well, I figured. That's why I never ask."

"This isn't never asking."

She looked at him, at the side of his head. He wouldn't look at her. "We've known each other for seven years, Zack."

"And I'm sure I don't know everything about you, either. But I know what counts. I know that you lick the mixer. Even if it's got batter with raw eggs on it."

She laughed. "Tell anyone that and I'll ruin you."

"I have no doubt. I also know that you like stupid comedies."

"And I know that you put on football games and never end up watching them. You're just in it for the snacks."

He smiled, his gray eyes meeting hers. "See? You know the real truth."

Except there was something in the way he said it, a strange undertone, that told her she didn't. She wasn't sure how she'd missed it before. But she had. Now it seemed blatant, obvious. Zack had a way of presenting such a calm, easy front. In business, she knew it was to disarm, that no matter how easygoing he appeared, he was the man in charge. No question.

Now she wondered how much of the easy act in his personal life was just that. An act.

His eyes lingered on her face for a moment, and she suddenly became acutely conscious of her lips. And how dry they were. She stuck out the tip of her tongue and moistened them, the action taking an undertone she hadn't intended when she'd begun.

This week was going to kill her. Eventually the tension would get too heavy and she would be crushed beneath the weight of it. There was no possible way she could endure any more.

"I'm really tired," she said, the lie so blatant and obvious it was embarrassing.

To Zack's credit, he didn't call her on it. "The inner sanctum is all yours. I'll make do with the couch."

She wasn't going to feel bad about that for a second. "All right, I'll see you in the morning."

Maybe by morning some of the surrealism of the whole day

would have worn off. Maybe by morning she wouldn't feel choked by the attraction she felt to Zack.

Maybe, but not likely.

CHAPTER FIVE

"Mr. Amudee has extended an invitation for you and me to have a private tour of the forest land."

Zack strode into the kitchen area and Clara sucked coffee down into her lungs. He was wearing jeans, only jeans, low on his lean hips, his chest bare and muscular and far too tempting. She could lean right in and...

"Coffee for me?" he asked.

"Oh, yes. Sure." She picked up the carafe and poured some coffee into a bright blue mug. "It's the shade-grown Chiang Mai Morning Blend. Really good. Strong but bright, a bit of citrus."

"I love it when you talk coffee to me," he said, lifting the mug to his lips, a wicked grin curving his mouth.

There was something borderline domestic about the scene. Although, nothing truly domestic could have such a dangerous, arousing edge to it, she was certain. And Zack, shirtless, had all of those things.

"All right, tell me about the tour," she said, looking very hard into her coffee mug.

"Very romantic. For the newly engaged."

Her stomach tightened. "Great."

"I hope you brought a swimsuit."

Oh, good. Zack in a swimsuit. With her in a swimsuit. That was going to help things get back on comfortable footing. She looked at Zack, at the easy expression on his handsome face. The ridiculous thing was, the footing was perfectly comfortable for him. Her little hell of sexual frustration was one hundred percent private. All her own. Zack wasn't remotely ruffled.

Typical.

"Yes, I brought a swimsuit."

"Good. I'll meet you back here in twenty minutes."

"Right." Unfortunately it would take longer than twenty minutes to plot an escape. So that meant Zack and swimsuits.

She tried to ignore the small, eternally optimistic part of her that whispered it might be a good thing.

Clara tugged at her brilliant pink sarong and made sure the knot was secure at her breasts before stepping out into the courtyard, where Zack was standing already.

"Ready. What's the deal? Give."

"You have to wait and see," he said, moving behind her, placing his hand low on her back as he led her to the gate and out onto a narrow path that wound through a thick canopy of trees and opened on an expansive green lawn.

"Are you kidding me?" she asked, stopping, her eyes widening.

There were two elephants in the field, one equipped with a harness that had small, cushioned seats on top. He was large enough he looked like he could comfortably seat at least four.

"Elephant rides are a big tourist draw in Chiang Mai," Zack said, the corner of his mouth lifting. "And I've never done it before, so I thought I would take advantage of the offer."

"First time for you?" she asked. She'd intended it as a joke, but it hit a bit to close to that sexual undercurrent they'd been dealing with since they left San Francisco.

A slow smile spread across his face. "Just for the elephant ride."

"Right. Got it." She was sure she was turning pink.

"You?"

She just about choked. "The elephant?"

"What else would I have been asking about?"

Her virginity. Except, no he wouldn't have been asking about that. It wasn't like she had a neon sign on her forehead that blinked red and said Virgin on it. Unless she did. Maybe he could tell.

She really hoped he couldn't tell.

"Yes, first time on an elephant," she said drily, aiming for cool humor. She wasn't sure she made her mark, but it was a valiant effort.

"Mr. Parsons." There was a man in white linen pants and a loose white shirt approaching them, his hand raised in greeting. "Ms. Davis, I believe," he said, stopping in front of her, his dark eyes glittering with warmth.

"Yes," Clara said, extending her hand. He bent his head and dropped a kiss on it, smiling, the skin around his eyes wrinkling with the motion.

"Isra Amudee. Pleasure." He straightened and shook Zack's hand. "Very glad you could make it. Especially after what happened."

Zack put his arm around Clara's waist and Clara tried to ignore the jolt of heat that raced through her. "Really, it didn't take me long to discover it wasn't a problem. Clara...well, I've known her for a long time. I don't really know how I missed what was right in front of me."

Mr. Amudee's smile widened. "A new wedding in your future, then?"

Zack stiffened. "Naturally. Actually I've already asked."

"And she's accepted?" Amudee looked at her and Clara felt her stomach bottom out.

Zack tightened his hold on her. "Yes," she said, her throat sandpaper dry. "Of course."

"And you, I bet, will have the good sense to show up. Now, I'll leave you to the elephants. I have to go and take a walk around the grounds. But I'll see you later on."

Clara watched Amudee walk away and tried to ignore the buzzing in her head as the man who was with the elephants introduced himself in English as Joe. He explained how the ride would work, that the elephant knew the route through the forrest and up to a waterfall, and she wouldn't deviate from that.

"They're trained. Very well. Safe. You'll be riding Anong." Joe indicated the elephant who was harnessed up. "And I'll follow on Mali. Just as a precaution."

He tapped Anong on her back leg and she bent low, making it easy for them to climb up onto the seat. Zack went first, then leaned forward and extended his hand, helping her up onto the bench.

"Seat belts," he said, raising one eyebrow as he fastened the long leather strap over both of their laps.

"Comforting," she said, a tingle of nerves and excitement running through her.

"Ready?" their guide called to them.

"I have no idea," she whispered to Zack.

"Ready," Zack said.

The elephant rose up, the sharp pitch forward and to the left a shock. She lurched to the side and took hold of Zack's arm while Anong finished getting to her feet, each movement throwing them in a different direction.

"I think I'm good now," she whispered, her fingers still wrapped, clawlike around Zack's arm.

"Just relax, he said this is a path she takes all the time. New for us, but not new for her."

She didn't actually want to know the answer to the question, but she asked it anyway. "Accustomed to calming the nerves of the inexperienced?"

"No. I don't mess around with women who need comforting in the bedroom. That's not what I'm there for."

She felt a heavy blush spread over her cheeks. "I guess not."

She was alternately relieved and disappointed by that bit

of news. Relieved, because she didn't really like to think of her friend as some crass seducer of innocents, and she really couldn't picture him in that role, anyway.

If he was the big bad wolf, it would be because the woman he was with wanted to play Little Red Riding Hood.

But it was disappointing, too, because that pushed her even farther outside the box that Zack's "ideal woman" resided in.

Ideal bedmate.

Sure, maybe it was more that than any sort of romantic ideal, but she would like to just fit the requirements for that. Well, really, being the woman he was sleeping with was very far away from what she actually wanted, but it would be a start.

A wonderful, sexual, amazing start...

She jerked her thoughts back to the present, not hard to do with the pitch-and-roll gait of the elephant rivaling a storm-tossed boat. It was a smooth, fluid sort of motion, but it was a very big motion, to match the size of the animal.

It also wasn't hard to do when she remembered that, as far as their host was concerned, she and Zack were now engaged.

"A tangled web, isn't it, Parsons?" she asked.

"What was I supposed to say?" he countered. "Ah, no, this is just my best friend that I brought along for a roll in the hay."

"The truth might have worked. He seems like a nice man."

"Look, it's done. I'm sure his assumption works even more in my favor, in favor of the deal, and that's all that really matters, right? We know where we stand. It's not like it changes anything between us."

She felt like the air had been knocked out of her. "No. Of course not."

They moved through the meadow and down into the trees, onto a well-worn path that took them along a slow-moving river, the banks covered in greenery, bright pink flowers glowing from the dark, lush foliage.

She tried to keep her focus on the view, but her mind kept wandering back to Zack, to his solid, steady heat, so close to her. It would be easy to just melt into him, to stop fighting so hard for a moment and give in to the need to touch him.

But she wouldn't. She couldn't. Nothing had changed between them, after all. His words.

There was a reason she'd never made any sort of attempt to change their relationship from friends to more-than-friends. The biggest one being that she didn't want to jeopardize the most stable relationship she had, the one closest to it being unable to stomach the thought of being rejected by him.

Of having him confirm that everything her mother said about her was true. Of having her know, for certain, that a man really wouldn't want her because she just wasn't all that pretty. Her mother had made sure she'd known men would still sleep with her, because of course, men would sleep with anyone. But she wasn't the sort of woman a man would want for a wife. Not the type of woman a man could be proud to take to events.

Not like her sister. Gorgeous, perfect Lucy who was, in all unfairness, smart and actually quite sweet along with being slender, blonde and generally elegant.

Lucy actually would have looked more like Hannah's sister than like *her* sister.

A sobering thought, indeed.

She should make sure Zack never met her sister.

The sound of running water grew louder and they rounded a curve in the path and came into a clearing that curved around a still, jade pool. At least twenty fine steams were trickling down moss-covered rocks, meeting at the center and falling into the pool as one heavy rush of water.

Anong the elephant stopped at the edge of the pool, dropping slowly down to her knees, the ground rising up a bit faster than Clara would have like. She leaned into Zack, clinging to the sleeve of his T-shirt as Anong settled.

"All right?" he asked.

She looked at where her hand was, and slowly uncurled her fingers, releasing her hold on him. "Sorry," she said.

He smiled, that simple expression enough to melt her insides. He was so sexy. Time and exposure, familiarity, didn't change it. Didn't lessen it.

Just another reason for her to leave Roasted. If exposure didn't do it, distance might.

Zack moved away from her, dismounting their ride first and waited for her at the side of their living chariot, his hand outstretched. She leaned forward and took it, letting his muscles propel her gently to the ground. Her feet hit just in front of his, her breasts close to touching his chest, the heat from him enticing her, taunting her.

"Do you want me to wait for you?" their guide asked.

Zack shook his head. "We'll walk back. Thank you for the ride. It was an experience."

He nodded and whistled a signal to Anong, who rose slowly and turned, going back with her owner and friend. She watched them round the corner, a smile on her lips. Yesterday, she was at a beachside hotel in San Francisco, expecting to lose half of her heart as Zack married another woman.

Today she was with him on his honeymoon. Riding elephants.

"An experience," Zack said, turning to face the water.

"It was fun," she said.

"Not relaxing exactly."

"No," she said, laughing. "Not in the least."

"Mr. Amudee informed me by phone this morning that this is a safe place to swim. Clean. They don't let the elephants up here and the waterfall keeps it all moving."

She made a face. "Good to know. I liked the elephants, don't really want to share a swimming hole with them. It looks pristine," she said, moving to the edge, looking down into the clear pool. She could see rocks covered in moss along the bottom, small fish darting around, only leaving the cover of their hiding places for a few moments before swimming behind something else. "Perfect."

Zack tugged his black shirt over his head, leaving him in nothing more than a pair of very low-cut white board shorts that, when wet, she had no doubt would cling to some very interesting places.

Her mind was a filthy place lately. And the sad thing was, it was hard to regret. Because it was so enjoyable.

"Swimming?"

"No." She shook her head and gripped her sarong.

"Why?"

"It looks cold."

He put his hands on his lean hips and sighed, the motion making his ab muscles ripple in a very enticing fashion. "It's so hot and muggy out here it could be snowmelt and it would feel good. And I guarantee you it's not snowmelt."

"It just looks...cold." Lame. So lame. But she didn't really want to strip down to her swimsuit in front of him, not when he looked so amazing in his. She was... There was too much of her for a start. She was so very conscious of that. Of the fact that she had hips and breasts, and that she could pinch fat on her stomach.

Zack's girlfriends had hip bones and abs that were just as cut as his.

"Ridiculous." He walked over to her and scooped her up in his arms, her heart climbing up into her throat as he did. His arms were tight and strong around her, masculine. Lifting her seemed effortless. His large hands cupped her thigh and her shoulder, his heat spreading through her like warm, sticky honey, thick and sweet.

She realized what was happening a little bit too late, because sexual attraction had short-circuited her brain. She put her hand flat on his chest, another bolt of awareness shocking her even as Zack took two big steps off the bank and down into the water.

The hot and cold burst through her, her body still warm from his touch on the inside, the water freezing her skin.

"Zack!"

He looked down at her, smiling. She sputtered and clung to his shoulders, his arms still wrapped tightly around her. His skin was slick now, so sexy, and it took everything in her arsenal of willpower to keep from sliding her palms down from their perch on his shoulders and flattening them against his amazing, perfect pecs.

She wanted to. She wanted to press her lips to the hollow of his throat, lick the water drops that were clinging to his neck.

She wiggled against him and managed to extricate herself from his grasp. Fleeing temptation.

She walked up to the shallow part of the pool, her pink sarong limp and heavy now, clinging to her curves like a second skin. She untied it and looped it over a tree branch. There was no point in it now.

She felt exposed in her black one-piece. It was pretty modest by some suit standards, but anything that tight tended to make her feel a bit exposed.

"Well, that's one way to get me in the water. Brute force," she sniffed, walking back to the water and sinking into the depths quickly, desperate for the covering it would provide.

"Brute?" Zack swam to where she was, treading water, his eyes glinting with amusement.

"Uh...yeah. You took advantage of me."

He paddled closer, his face a whisper from hers. "I didn't take advantage of you. If I had, you'd have known it, that's for sure."

Strangely, with her body half submerged in water, her throat suddenly felt bone-dry. "I feel um...taken advantage... You... picked me up and threw me in and I'm...wet."

His expression changed, his eyes darkening. "Interesting."

"Oh, *pffft*." She dunked her head, letting the cold water envelop her, pull the stinging heat from her cheeks. She paddled toward the waterfall, away from Zack. Away from certain mortification and temptation.

She surfaced again and looked back at Zack, still treading water where she'd left him.

Nice, Clara. Next time just tell him straight up that you're hot for him and would like to jump him, if that's all right with him.

She pulled a face for her own benefit and climbed up one of the mossy rocks that sat beneath the slow flowing falls, water trickling down, mist hovering above the surface of the cool, plant-covered stones.

She pulled her knees to her chest and looked up, squinting at the sunlight pouring through the thick canopy of trees.

"You're like a jungle fairy."

She looked down into the water and saw Zack, his hair wet and glistening.

"You're startling me," she said. More with his statement than with his presence, but she didn't intend to elaborate.

He planted his palms flat on the rocks and hoisted himself up, the muscles in his shoulders rolling and shifting with the motion. He sat next to her, the heat from his body a welcome respite from the cold. But that was about all it was a respite from. Because mostly he just made her feel edgy.

And happy. He made her so happy that it hurt. Just being with him made everything seem right. Like a missing part of herself was finally in place. Like some of her insecurities and inadequacies didn't matter so much.

And that was just stupid. Not to mention scary. Because it was an illusion. He would never be with her in the way she wanted, and watching him marry another woman, give someone else everything she longed for, *that* would turn her happiness into the bitterest pain.

The kind she wasn't sure she could withstand.

"You're beautiful," he said.

She turned sharply to look at him, her heart in her throat. "What?"

"Just stating a fact."

"It's not one you typically state. About me, I mean."

He put his hand out and brushed a water drop from her cheek with his thumb, the motion sending an electric shock through her body, heat pooling in her stomach and radiating from there to her limbs.

"Well, I thought it needed to be said."

It was so tantalizingly close to what she wanted. But to him it was simply an empty compliment, or maybe he even meant it. But not in the way she would. He didn't mean she was beautiful in the same way she found him beautiful. The way that made her body warm and her heart flutter.

"Thanks for that. You aren't so bad, either." She tried to sound casual. Light. Like a friend. Like she was supposed to sound.

He smiled and lifted his arm, curling his fist in, showing off his very, very impressive biceps.

"You're shameless," she said, somehow managing to laugh around her stubborn heart, still lodged firmly in her throat.

"Sorry."

"About as sorry as you are for dumping me in the water?"

"Yeah. About." He leaned in, his arm curving around her waist and everything slowed down for a moment. He tightened his hold on her, his face so close...

And then they were falling.

She shrieked just before they hit the water. And surfaced with a loud curse, unreasonable anger mingling with disappointment. "Zack! You jackass!"

She moved to him and planted her hands on his shoulders, attempting to dunk him beneath the water. He put his hands on her waist and held her still in front of him, her movements impotent against his strength.

"You can touch bottom here, can't you?" she asked, her feet

hovering above the sandy floor of the pool while Zack seemed firmly rooted.

"Maybe."

His hands slipped down, resting on her hips, the heat from his touch cutting through the icy chill in the water. He kept one hand there, the other sliding around to her back, his fingers drifting upward, skimming the line of her spine.

She shivered, but she wasn't cold. And he didn't let go.

His eyes were locked with hers, the head there matching the heat he was spreading over her skin. Her hands were still on his shoulders. And since he'd just moved his hands, it seemed... somehow it seemed right to move hers.

Her heart thundered in her chest as she slid her hands down, palms skimming his chest hair, the firm muscles beneath, as she rested them against his chest. She could hardly breathe. Her chest, her stomach, every last muscle, was too tightly wound.

His fingers flexed, the blunt tips digging into her flesh. His hands were rough, strong, everything she'd ever imagined and so much more.

Zack loosened his hold, a muscle in his jaw jerking. She pulled away from him, the water freezing where his hands had been.

"We should go," Zack said, his words abrupt.

"I... We haven't been here very long." She felt muddled, as though the mist from the waterfall had wrapped itself around her, making everything seem fuzzy.

And she was glad. Because she had a feeling that when the reality of what had just happened, of how stupid she'd been, hit, it was going to hit hard.

"Yes, but I have some things to take care of before tonight. We have dinner reservations at the restaurant down in the main part of the resort."

He reversed direction and swam to shore, walking out of the pool, his muscular legs fighting against the water pressure, his swim trunks conforming to his body. A hard pang hit her in the stomach when she looked and saw the outline of his erection. Had she really gotten him hot? Was that about her?

He turned away from her and pulled his shirt on.

And was the arousal why they were leaving now?

So he felt something. Even if he was running from it. Something that was at least physical.

Her hart hammered, echoing in her head, making her temples pulse.

Maybe she did matter to him, like that, at least a little bit? Maybe… Yes, she knew men were excited by women but this had to be personal. It had to be about her, at least a little bit. Did he think she was sexy?

She followed him to shore, scrambling onto the sandy ground, her feet picking up grains of dirt, clinging to her toes. She shook her foot out, grateful to have something else to concentrate on for a moment.

She looked back up and saw Zack, his eyes on her, his jaw locked tight.

She swallowed hard and grabbed her sarong. "So we're having dinner out tonight?"

"Yes," he bit out. "I have to go and pick up a package down in town and then I'll meet you back up at the villa. The car will be by around seven."

"Okay." She wished she could come up with something better than the bland, one-word answer, but she just couldn't.

Something had changed. The air around them seemed tight, the way Zack looked at her new and strange. And for the first time, she felt power in her beauty, in her body.

And she wondered if maybe he could want her. If she could be the sort of woman he wanted.

Maybe tonight she would actually try.

It was criminal. The dress that Clara was wearing should be illegal. She certainly shouldn't be allowed out in public. It was tight, like that black, second-skin swimsuit, accentuating curves that, until this afternoon, he hadn't realized were quite so...lush.

Breasts that were round and perfect, firm looking. They would overflow in his hands. And her hips were incredible, nothing like the androgynous, straight up-and-down supermodels that were so in style. Not even like Hannah, whose image he was having trouble conjuring up.

Today, at the river, with her body pressed against his, wet and slick, soft and feminine, he'd had a reaction he really hadn't counted on. He hadn't counted on touching her like he had, either. Exploring the elegant line of her back. Holding her to him. It had been a big mistake.

Getting out of the water, in front of his best friend, sporting an erection inspired by her, hadn't really been his idea of a good time.

He put his hand in his pocket, let his fingers close around the velvet box that was nestled there. The one that Hannah had had rush delivered to the resort. Because it was the right thing to do, or so she'd said. He hadn't really cared whether he got the engagement ring back or not. But he could use it.

The thing with Amudee, his assumption, had been unexpected. But Zack was good at reading people and the older man's delight at the thought had been so obvious, there had been no way he would disappoint him. Not with so much riding on things going well this week.

His other plans had all gone to hell. He wasn't sending this one there with the rest of them.

"What exactly is that?" he asked. They were in the car, being driven up to the main area of the resort, and being closed in with her when she looked like that and smelled, well, she smelled sweet enough to taste, was a bit of torture.

"What?" she asked.

"What you're wearing."

Her cheeks colored. "A dress."

"But do you...call it something?"

"A dress," she said again, her voice low now, dangerous.

"It's a nice dress."

She looked straight ahead. "Thank you."

The car stopped in front of an open, wooden building that had all the lights on despite the late hour. There were people sitting at a bar, musicians set down in the center of the seating area, and dancers out on the grass, candles balanced on their hands as they moved in time with the music.

He opened his door and Clara just sat, her posture stiff. "What?"

"Now I'm not sure if I should go back and change."

"I don't even want to understand women," he said.

"Why?"

"You just changed into that dress, so clearly you thought it was a good choice, and now you want to change back?"

"Because there must be something wrong with what I'm wearing. Although, you didn't seem to have a problem with my bathing suit, and it showed a lot more than this." She put a hand on her stomach. "It's too tight."

His body hardened. "Trust me, it's not. Every man in the bar is going to give himself whiplash when you walk by."

She frowned. "Really?"

She looked...mystified. Doubtful.

"Did you not look at yourself in the mirror?" he asked, completely incredulous that she somehow didn't see what he did. That she didn't realize how appealing a dress that was basically a second skin was to a man. It showed every bit of her shape, while still concealing the details. Made him feel desperate to see everything, the tease nearly unbearable.

She looked away from him. "That's the trouble, I did, and I chose to wear it anyway."

"What makes you think it doesn't look good?"

"You reacted...funny."

"Because I'm not used to seeing so much of you. But what I can see is certainly good."

"Really?"

He took a lock of her silky hair between his thumb and fore-finger. A mistake. It was so soft. Like he imagined the rest of her would be. "Didn't I tell you any man would put up with your snoring for the pleasure of having you sleep with him?"

His eyes dropped to her mouth and he felt an uncomfortable shock of sensation when, for the second time in the past hour, she stuck her pink tongue out and slicked it across her lips, leaving them looking glossy and oddly kissable.

Clara felt like there was someone sitting on her chest, keeping her from breathing. The knot of insecurity that had tied up her stomach was changing into something else, something dangerous. A strand of hope she had no business feeling. A kind of feminine pride that didn't make sense.

Zack was a charmer. He could charm the white gloves off a spinster, and what he was saying to her was no different. Empty charm that had no real weight behind it. It was easy to say that some other man would like to share her bed. It didn't mean he did. Or that anyone he even knew would.

All right, in reality, she knew how men were about sex. If she was willing to put out they wouldn't care if she had a pinch of extra flesh around her middle, but that wasn't really the issue. She didn't want to be a second choice. Second best.

She was even second-guessing the physical reaction Zack had had to her down at the river. Because that could simply be a man overdue for sex. Nothing more. She'd made it personal because she'd been desperate for it. But in reality, he was supposed to be here, with his wife, having lots and lots of sex, and he wasn't. But she doubted he'd forgotten.

She was tired of being in the shadow of someone else. Even tonight, she was the consolation prize for Zack. Rather than spending the night with Hannah, he was with her, watching traditional dancing instead of having hot, sweaty, wedding night sex. Ah, yes, all fine and good for him to say those things to her, but he wasn't really backing it up.

She forced a smile. "You did. All right, let's go...drink or something."

He chuckled. "Sounds like a good idea to me."

They both got out of the car and walked over to an alcove, shrouded in misty fabric, like everything in the whole resort property. It was designed for people to take advantage of the perceived privacy. It was an invitation to some sort of heady, fantastic sin. Traditional values her fanny.

She sat down on one of the cushions, positioned in front of a low table. Zack sat next to her, so close she could feel the heat radiating off his body.

"So what about my comment spawned the dress edition of twenty questions?" he asked.

"I don't usually wear things that are this tight, so you...your reaction made me think it looked... You've met my mother, right?" She changed tactics.

"Yes."

"She's like a model. And my sister...well, she takes after my mom. I take after my dad."

"Something wrong with that?"

"Well, I'm just not...not everything Lucy is. And my mother let me know that. Let me know that I was second best in nearly every way. She didn't just get beauty, she had a perfect grade-point average without even trying. I was just average. I liked school, but I didn't excel at it. The only thing I've ever excelled at is baking, which in my mother's estimation contributes to my weight issues."

Zack swore and Clara jumped. "Weight issues? You don't have weight issues."

"I did. More than I do now, I mean. It was a whole...thing in high school. Remember, I mentioned the time my date stood me up?"

He nodded and she continued on, hating to dredge up the memory. "Asking me was a joke in the first place, not that I had any idea, of course. And I was supposed to meet him by the stage in the gym, which is where the dance was, and he walked up with his real date, and the guys doing the lights knew to put a spotlight on me right then. And I was all chubby and wrapped up in this silly, tight pink dress that was just so... shiny. That stays with you. Sometimes, for no reason, I still feel like the girl under the spotlight, with everyone looking at all my flaws."

He swore sharply. "That's bull. That's...kids are stupid and that's high school." He swallowed. "It's not real life. None of us stay the same as we were back then." His words ended sounding rough, hard.

"Maybe not. Still, even though I've sort of...slimmed out as I've grown up, as far as my mom is concerned, since I'm not six feet tall and runway ready, I'm not perfect. I have her genes, too, after all," she said, echoing a sentiment she'd heard so many times. "And that means I could be much thinner if I *tried.*"

"Let me tell you something about women's bodies, Clara, and I know you are a woman, but I'm still going to claim the greater expertise. Men like women's bodies, and there isn't only one kind to like, that's part of the fun. Beauty isn't just one thing."

She tried to ignore the warm, glowy feeling that was spreading through her. "I know that. I mean, part of me knows that. But it's hard to let go of the second-best thing."

"Better than feeling like you're above everyone else," he said slowly. "Like nothing can touch you because you're just so damn perfect life wouldn't dare."

"I don't know if Lucy feels that way, my mother might but..." She trailed off when she noticed the look on his face. There was something, just for a moment, etched there that was so cold, so utterly filled with despair that it reached inside her and twisted her heart.

"Zack..."

He shook his head. "Nothing, Clara. Just leave it." The dancers had cleared the area out on the lawn and there were couples moving out into the lit circles, holding each other close, looking at each other with a kind of longing that made Clara ache with jealousy. "Care to dance before dinner is served?"

Yes and no. She felt a bit too fragile to be so close to him, and yet a part of her wanted it more than she wanted air. Just like in the water today, she'd wanted to run and cling at the same time. She was never sure which desire would win out.

He offered his hand and she took it, his fingers curling around hers, warm and masculine. He helped her up from her seat and drew her to him, his expression still strange, foreign more than familiar. He looked leaner, more dangerous. Which was strange, because even though Zack was her friend, she always felt an edge of danger around him, a little bit of unrest. Probably because she was so attracted to him that just looking at him made her shiver with longing.

"Just a warning," he said, as they made their way out onto the grass. "People will probably stare. But that's because you look good, amazing even. And you certainly aren't second to any woman here."

"Flatterer."

"No, I'm not, and I think we both know that."

"Okay, I suppose that's true," she said, kicking her shoes off and enjoying the feeling of the grass under her feet. Although, losing the little lift her shoes provided put her eyes level with Zack's chest.

He pulled her to him, his hand on her waist. She fought the urge to melt into him, to rest her head on his chest. This wasn't that kind of dance; theirs wasn't that kind of relationship. That didn't mean she didn't want to pretend. It was easy, with the heat of his body so close to hers, to imagine that tonight might end differently. To imagine that he saw her as a woman.

Not just in the way that he'd referenced, that vague, sweet, but generic talk about women and their figures. But that he would desire her body specifically. She kept her eyes open, fixed on his throat. She knew him so well, that even looking there she knew just who she was with. And she didn't want to shut that reality out by closing her eyes. She wanted to watch, relish.

For a moment reality seemed suspended. There wasn't time, there wasn't a fiancée, one more suited to Zack than she was, looming in the background. There was only her and Zack, the heat of the night air, the strains from the stringed instruments weaving around them, creating a sensual, exotic rhythm that she wanted to embrace completely.

She loved him so much.

That hit her hard in the chest. The final, concrete acknowledgment of what she'd probably always known. A moment that was completely lacking in denial for once. She loved Zack. With her entire heart, with everything in her. And she was in his arms now.

But not in the way she wanted to be. She breathed in deeply, smelling flowers, rain and Zack. Her lungs burned, her stomach aching. She wished it was real. So much that it hurt, down to her bones.

Maybe, just for a moment, she could pretend that it was real. That this was romance. That he held her because he wanted her. Because after this, after the fake engagement, after the ink was dry on the contracts, there would be no more chances to pretend.

She would go her way, and she would leave Zack behind. Why couldn't she ignore it now? Just for now.

She didn't want the song to end, wished the notes would linger in the air forever, an excuse to stay in his arms. But it ended. And that was why she shouldn't have said yes to the dance in the first place. Playing games wouldn't come close to giving her what she wanted with Zack. It just made her aware of how far she was from having what she really wanted.

He took her hand and pulled her away from the other dancing couples, and for one heart-stopping moment, she thought he might lean in and kiss her. His lips were close to hers, his breath hot, fanning across her cheek. Her body felt too tight, her skin too hot. She needed something. Needed him.

"I have something for you," he said. "For tomorrow."

"I like presents," she said, trying to keep her voice from sounding too shaky. Too needy. Too honest. "It's not a food processor, is it?"

He chuckled, a low, sexy sound that reverberated through her. "I told you, I'm keeping my food processor."

She tried to breathe. "All right then, I can't guess."

He reached into his jacket pocket and pulled out a small velvet box. Everything slowed down for a moment, but unlike before, when the gauzy, frothy film of fantasy had covered it all, this was stark reality. She shook her head even before he opened it, but he didn't seem to notice.

He popped the top on it and revealed a huge ring, glittering gold and diamonds. She sucked in a sharp breath. Such a perfect ring. Gorgeous. Extravagant. Familiar. The ring he'd given to Hannah. The exact same ring. The ring for the woman who was supposed to be here. The ring for the woman he should have danced with, the woman he would have kissed, made love to.

A well of pain, deep, unreasonable and no less intense for it, opened up in her, threatened to consume her. What a joke. A cheap trick. And the worst part was that she'd played it on herself. Letting herself pretend that he'd wanted *her* at the river, playing like he wanted her in his arms tonight.

Letting hope exist in her, along with the futile, ridiculous love she felt for him. Ridiculous, because for half a second, her breath had caught when she'd seen the ring, and she'd forgotten it was fake.

"No," she said.

"Clara…"

"I don't…" She was horrified to feel wetness on her cheeks, tears falling she hadn't even realized were building. She backed away from him, hitting her shoulder against one of the bar area's supporting pillars. But she didn't stop. "I'm sorry."

She wasn't sorry. She was angry. She was hurt. Ravaged to her soul. Maybe it had been ignorant of her not to think all the way to the ring. To think that the farce wouldn't include that. Of course it would. Zack didn't cut corners and he didn't forget details. So of course he wouldn't forget something as essential to an engagement as a ring.

But it hurt. To see him, impossibly gorgeous and, in so many ways, everything she'd always dreamed of, offering her a ring, a ring he'd already given to another woman, as part of a lie, it killed something inside her.

Maybe it was just the fact that it pulled her deepest, most secret fantasy out of her and laid it bare. And made it into a joke. Designed to show her that there was no way he would ever consider her. Not with any real seriousness. That she was nothing more than a replacement for the woman he'd intended to have here with him.

That she was interchangeable.

She was hopeless. She needed a friend to tell her what a head case she was. To tell her to get over him. To take her out to pie and tell her she could do better, have better.

But Zack should have been that person. *He* was her best friend. He was the one she talked to. The one she confided in. And she couldn't confide this, couldn't tell him that he'd just shredded her heart. Couldn't tell him she was hopelessly in love with a man she couldn't have, because he was the man.

The crushing loneliness that thought brought on, the pain, was overwhelming.

Her stomach twisted. "I have to… I'm sorry."

She turned away from him, walking quickly across the lawn, back to into the lobby area to find a car, an elephant, whatever would get her back to the villa the fastest.

She was running and she knew it. From him. From her hurt. And from the moment she knew would come, the one where she'd have to explain to him just why looking at the ring had made her cry.

It was an explanation she never wanted to give. Because the only man she could ever confide her pain in, was also the one man she could never tell. Because he was the man who'd caused it.

CHAPTER SIX

ZACK'S heart pounded as he scanned the villa's courtyard. It was too dark to see anything, but he was sure this was where she was. Unless she'd called the car service and asked them to come and get her, which, if Clara was really upset, he wouldn't put past her. She could be on the next plane back to the States.

His plane.

Which, he had a suspicion he might deserve.

There was a narrow path that led from the main area of the courtyard into an alcove surrounded by flowering plants and trees. And he was willing to bet that, if she was still in the villa, she'd gone there.

He was right. She was sitting on the stone bench, her knees pulled up to her chest. She was simply staring, her cheeks glistening in the moonlight. The sight made him ache.

He was all about control, all about living life with as few entanglements and attachments as possible. But Clara was his exception. She had been from the moment he'd met her.

She was the one person who could alter his emotions without his say so. Make him happy if he really wanted to be angry. Make his gut feel wrenched with her tears.

"Are you okay?"

She dropped her knees and put her feet on the ground, straightening. "I'm sorry. That was stupid. I overreacted."

He moved to the bench and crouched down in front of it, in front of her. "What did I do?"

"I was just…I told you, it was an overreaction. It was nothing, really." She sucked in a breath that ended on a hiccup and his heart twisted. "I can't really…explain it."

The confusion he felt was nearly as frustrating as the pain he felt over hurting her. He didn't really understand exactly what he'd done, but not understanding it didn't make it go away.

Without thinking, he lifted his hand and curved it around her neck, stroking her tender skin with his thumb. It was a gesture meant to comfort her, because he'd upset her somehow, for the second time in forty-eight hours, and he hated to upset her. She meant too much to him.

But something in the touch changed. He wasn't sure exactly when it tipped over from being comfort to being a caress, he wasn't sure how her skin beneath his fingers transformed from something everyday to something silky, tempting.

She looked at him, her eyes glistening, the expression in them angry. Angry and hot. And that heat licked through him, reached down into his gut and squeezed him tight.

It was close to what he'd felt down at the river, but magnified, her anger feeding the flame that burned between them. And he couldn't walk away from it. Not this time.

Without thought, without reason or planning, without stopping to think of possible consequences, he leaned in and closed the space between them, his lips meeting hers. First kisses were for tasting, testing. They were a question.

At least historically for him they had been. This kiss wasn't.

Something roared through him, filling him, a kind of desperation he'd never felt before. He didn't ask, he took. He didn't taste, he devoured. The hunger in him was too ravenous to do anything else, so sudden he had no chance to sublimate it. He wrapped his arms around her, and she clung to his shoulders, her lips parting beneath his.

He growled and thrust his tongue against hers, his body

shuddering as his world reduced to the slick friction, to the warmth of her lips on his.

Clara was powerless to do anything but cling to Zack. Powerless to give anything less than every bit of passion and desire that was pouring through her. To do anything but devour him, giving in to the hunger that had lived in her, gnawed at her for the past seven years.

This was heaven. And it was hell. Everything she'd longed for, still off-limits to her for the same reasons it always had been. Except for right now, for some reason, it was as though a ban had been lifted. For this one moment, a moment out of time. A moment that she needed more than she needed air.

His lips, firm and sure, were everything she'd ever dreamed they might be, his hands, heavy and hot on her back even more arousing than she'd thought possible.

This was why there had been no one else. Because the idea of Zack had always been more enticing than the reality of any other man. And the reality of Zack far surpassed any fantasy she'd ever had. Maybe any fantasy *any* woman had ever had.

She slid from the bench and onto the stone-covered ground, gripping the front of his shirt, their knees touching. He pulled her closer, bringing her breasts against his hard, muscular chest. She arched into him, craving more. Craving everything. All of him.

When they parted, he rested his forehead against hers, his breathing shallow, unsteady, loud in the otherwise silent night.

She didn't know what to say. She was afraid that he would try to say something first. Something that would ruin it. A joke. Or maybe he'd even be angry. Or he'd say it was a mistake. All valid reactions, but she didn't want any of them. She didn't want to deal with anything. She simply wanted to focus on the pounding of her heart, the swollen, tingly feeling in her lips. On all the really good, fizzy little sensations that were popping in her veins like champagne.

Zack let out a gust of air. "Damn."

She laughed. She couldn't help it. Of all the reactions she'd expected, and dreaded, that hadn't been it. That he would allow an honest reaction, and that his reaction would match hers, hadn't seemed likely.

"Yeah," she said.

He braced his hand on the bench behind her and pulled himself up, then extended his hand to her. She gripped it and let him help her to her feet. She brushed some dried leaves from her knees, ignoring the slight prickle of pain and indents of small twigs left behind on her skin.

Her eyes caught his and held, and all of the good exciting feelings that had been swirling through her dissolved. The cushion of fantasy yanked from under her, there was nothing but cold, hard reality. She'd kissed Zack. More than kissed, she'd attacked him.

And there was nowhere for it to go from that point. If she leaned in again, if she kissed him again, then what? They might go to bed together. And where would that leave her after? Where would it leave them?

No, he hadn't slept with Hannah, but he'd slept with other beautiful women. Lots of them. She'd met a good number of them. And she was…she was inexperienced, unglamorous. And she was here as a replacement. If something happened between them now, on a night that was meant to be his wedding night with another woman, she would always feel like she'd been second.

He was a man, and the pump was well and truly primed. He'd been promised sex after what had been a lengthy bout of not having sex, so of course he was hot for it. But he was hot for it. Not for her.

He'd never kissed her before tonight. That, if nothing else, cemented the point.

She wasn't going to cry again. She wasn't going to let him know how vulnerable she was to him. Wasn't going to let him know how bad it hurt to pull away now.

"This has been a bit of a crazy day," she said.

"I can't argue with that."

"Sorry. About this." She gestured to the bench. "All of it... I don't...I don't really know what that was about."

The flash of relief she saw in Zack's eyes made her heart twist. She would finish now. Make sure he'd never want to talk about it again.

"I mean...how do you feel?" She'd said the magic feel word. Zack didn't like to talk about how he felt. Not in a way that went any deeper than happy, or angry, or hungry.

"Fine. Good, in fact. Kissing a beautiful woman is never a bad thing."

She felt heat creep into her cheeks. She shouldn't respond to the compliment. It was empty, an attempt to smooth things over. But it affected her, and she couldn't stop it from making her stomach curl in traitorous satisfaction.

"I might say the same. Not the woman part but the... You get it."

"I did something wrong. With the ring. I'm sorry. I'm not hitting them out of the park with you today, am I?"

"I don't think either of us is at our best right now," she said. That at least was true. Of course, she hadn't been her best since the engagement announcement. Her safe little world had been chucked off-kilter in that moment and she'd felt out of balance ever since.

"Probably need sleep."

She forced a laugh. "You probably do. I got that extra sleep on the plane, remember?"

"But you should sleep again. Otherwise you'll be off for even longer."

She did feel tired suddenly. And not a normal tired, an all-consuming sort of tired that went all the way down into her bones. "Yeah. You're right. I can sleep on the couch tonight."

"I'll sleep on the couch again. After being left at the altar, sleeping alone in the honeymoon bed is just a bit depressing, don't you think?"

For a moment, she thought about inviting him to join her. To play the vixen for once. To say to hell with all of her insecurities and just be the woman she wished she could be.

But she didn't.

"Yeah, maybe a little." She swallowed and stuck her hand out. "I'll take that ring though."

"You sure?"

"I told you, I was being stupid. Emotional girl moment. The kind specifically designed to boggle the minds of men. Actually, a little secret for you, they occasionally boggle our minds, too. So, ring, give."

She held her hand out and he took it in his, turning it over so her palm was facing down. He took the ring box out of his pocket and took the ring out of its pink silk nest, holding it up for a moment before sliding it on to her ring finger.

She looked down at it, then curled her fingers into a fist, trying to force a smile.

"Looks good," he said.

"It's a diamond, it can't look anything else," she said, trying to sound breezy and unaffected. Both things she wasn't.

"Perfect. And now we're ready for tomorrow. I hope you brought shoes you can walk in."

"Of course I did."

"That's right. I forgot."

"Forgot what?" she asked.

"That you're different. Come on, let's go try to get some sleep."

She followed him out of the courtyard, trying to leave everything behind them, all the needs, desires, pain, back in the alcove. But his words kept repeating in her head, and she could still feel his kiss on her lips.

And she felt different. Like a completely different woman

than the one who had walked into the garden with tears streaming down her face.

One kiss shouldn't have that kind of power. But that kiss had. She felt changed. She felt a a tiny bit destroyed, and a little bit stronger. And she wasn't sure she would take it back. Even if she could.

Sleep had been a joke. An elusive thing that had never even come close to happening. Zack looked at the tie he'd brought with him for meetings with Mr. Amudee, and decided against putting it on. Not twice in one week.

He left two buttons undone on his crisp white shirt and pushed the sleeves halfway up his forearms. That should be good enough. They were spending the day looking at where the coffee and tea plants were grown.

Maybe spending the day outdoors would clear his head. Would lift the heavy fog of arousal that had plagued him since the kiss. Not just the kiss, since that strange, tense moment at the lake before the kiss.

But the kiss... A few more minutes and he would have had her flat on her back on the stone bench with more than half of her clothes stripped from her gorgeous curves.

He bit down hard, his teeth grinding together. He shouldn't be thinking of her curves. But he was.

"Zack?"

The sound of her voice hit him like a kick in the gut.

"Here," he said, sliding his belt through the loops on his pants and fastening the buckle as she walked around the corner, into the bedroom. Her pale cheeks colored slightly when she saw him.

"How did you sleep?" she asked.

"Great," he lied. "Thanks for letting me use the room to get ready."

"Yeah, no problem. I got up pretty early. Wandered around in the garden. There are so many flowers here."

And she'd put a few different varieties in her hair. It was silly. And it was cute. She had a way of making that work for her.

"I didn't know you liked flowers so much."

She shrugged. "I always have some on my kitchen table."

She did, now that he thought about it. He wondered if anyone ever bought them for her. He wondered why he'd never really stopped to notice before. Why he'd never bought her any.

Because, bosses don't buy employees flowers. And friends don't buy friends flowers.

Friends also didn't kiss each other like he and Clara had done last night. His pulse jump-started at the thought, his blood rushing south. He tightened his hands into fists and tried to will his body back under control.

"Ready to go?" he asked, his voice curt because it was taking every last bit of his willpower to keep his desire for her leashed.

She frowned slightly. "Yeah. Ready."

"Good. Remember, you're my fiancée, and we've been very suddenly overcome by love that can no longer be denied."

One side of her mouth quirked up. "Is that the story?"

"Yes. That's the story. As Amudee created it, so he'll believe it. He's the one who assumed."

"A romantic, I suppose. Either that or he just thinks you move fast."

"I'm decisive. And we've known each other for years." He studied her face for a moment, dark almost almond-shaped eyes, pale skin, clear and smooth. Perfection. Her lips were pink and full and, now he knew, made for kissing. And he had to wonder how he'd known her for so long and never really looked at her.

Because if he had he would have realized. He would have had to realize, that she was the most gorgeous woman. Exquisite. Curved, just as a woman should be, in all the right places. Beautiful without fuss or pretension.

"Yes, we have," she said slowly, those liquid brown eyes locked with his.

"So it stands to reason that after Hannah decided not to go through with things…"

"Right."

The air between them seemed thicker now, that dangerous edge sharpening. Now that he knew what it was like to touch her, to feel her soft lips beneath his, well, now it was a lot harder to ignore.

"So let's go, then," he said.

"Right," she said again.

He moved to her and slid his arm around her waist. It was more slender than he'd imagined it might be. "We have to do things like this," he said, his voice getting rougher as her hips brushed against his.

She nodded, her eyes on his face. On his lips. She would be the death of him.

"Lovely to see you again, Ms. Davis," Mr. Amudee said, inclining his head. "And with a ring, I see."

Her heart rate kicked up several notches.

"Oh. Yes. Zack…made it official last night. It's lovely to see you, too." She touched the ring on her finger and Zack tightened his hold around her waist. She nearly stopped breathing, her accelerated heart rate lurching to a halt with it. From the moment they'd arrived at Mr. Amudee's house, he had put his arm around her and kept it there. She'd assumed she would get used to it, to the warm weight of his touch. But she wasn't getting used to it. If anything, she was getting more jittery, more aroused with each passing second.

The sun was hot on the wide, open veranda that overlooked rows of coffee trees with flat glossy leaves and bright red coffee cherries. But Zack's touch was the thing that was making her melt.

"I had not met the other woman you intended to marry,

Zack, but I must say that comparing the photos of the first one, to Ms. Davis, I find I prefer Ms. Davis."

Clara's heart bumped against her chest. "That's kind of you to say." She knew her face had to be beet-red, it was hot, that was for sure. Because it was nice of him to say, but there was no way it could be true.

There was no comparison between her and Hannah. Hannah was...well, sex bomb came to mind yet again.

"Not kind," Isra said. "Just the truth. I was married, a long time ago, to the most wonderful woman. I have a good judge of character. Unfortunately I was too busy to see just how wonderful she was. Don't make that mistake."

Zack cleared his throat. "Clara is also very knowledgable about our product. I know we'll both enjoy getting a look at the growing process today. And we're both excited about the tasting."

Back to business. Zack was good at that. Thank God one of them was.

"I'm excited to share it with you. Come this way." They followed him down the stairs that led to the lush, green garden filled with fragrant foliage. He moved quickly for a man his age, his movements sharp and precise as he explained where each plant was in the growing stage, and which family was leasing which segment of the farmland, and how the soil and amount of shade would affect the flavor of each type of coffee, even before it was roasted.

The tea was grown in a more remote segment of the farm and required walking up into the rolling hills, where the leaves were in the process of being harvested.

"A lot depends on when you pick them," Mr. Amudee said, bending and plucking a small, tender-looking cluster of leaves. "Smell. Very delicate."

He handed the leaves to Zack and he did as instructed. Then he held them out for Clara. She bent and took in the light fragrance. She looked up and her eyes clashed with Zack's and her heart beat double time.

"And this will be…what sort of tea will it be?" she asked, anything to get her mind off Zack and his eyes.

"White tea," Zack said. "Am I right?"

Mr. Amudee inclined his head. "Right. Ready to go and taste?"

Her eyes met Zack's again, the word tasting bringing to mind something new and different entirely. Something heady and sexual.

She swallowed hard.

"Yes, I think we are," Zack said slowly, his eyes never leaving hers.

And she wondered if he'd been thinking the exact same thing she was. And if he was thinking the same thing, if he wanted to kiss her again, she wasn't sure what she would do.

No, that was a lie. She was sure. She would kiss him again. Like nothing else mattered. Like there was no future and no consequences. Because she'd had enough of not getting what she wanted out of life. Quite enough.

She looked at Zack again and she wondered if she'd only imagined that momentary flash of heat. Because his eyes were cool again, his expression neutral.

She tried to convince herself that it was better that way.

Clara spent the next few days carefully avoiding Zack. It was easier than expected, given the cozy living situation. But during the day he had meetings with Mr. Amudee and when she wasn't needed, she took advantage of all the vacation-type things that were available in the resort.

There was a spa down in the hotel, and also some incredible restaurants. Her favorite retreat was up on the roof of the villa that gave her a view of the mountains, and the small town that was only a short walk away, the golden rooftops reflecting the sunlight like fire in the late afternoon. It was the perfect view for yoga, which kept her mind focused and relaxed at the same time.

She even managed to forget about the kiss. Mostly. As long as she made a concerted effort not to think of it. And as long as she didn't get into bed before she was ready to fall asleep instantly. Lying awake for any length of time was a recipe for disaster. And for replaying that moment. Over and over again.

Clara took a deep breath and tried to focus on the scenery, on the sky as it lightened. Orange fading into a pale pink, then to purple as the sun rose from behind the sloping hills. She would focus on that. Not Zack. Because that door was clearly closed. He hadn't touched her again, unless it was absolutely necessary, since the night in the garden. Since the kiss that had scorched her inside and out.

The kiss that didn't even seem to be a vague memory to him.

"Got plans for today?"

She turned and her heart lodged itself in her throat. Zack strode onto the roof in nothing more than a pair of low-slung jeans, his chest, broad and muscular, sprinkled with the perfect amount of chest hair, was streaked with dirt and glistening with sweat.

She had to remind herself to breathe when he came closer. And she had to remind herself not to stare at his abs, bunching and shifting as he moved.

"Do I…" She blinked and looked up at his face. "What?"

"Do you have plans? You've been busy. Remarkably so for someone on vacation."

"Well, down in the village they have these neat classes for tourists. Weaving and things like that. And one of the restaurants in the hotel has a culinary school."

"I thought you wanted to relax."

"Cooking is relaxing for me." And it had been conducive to avoiding him. "Anyway, now I can make you some killer Pad Thai when we get back home."

"Well, I support that."

"What are you doing up so early?"

"Working. Before the sun had a chance to get over the mountains and scorch me. Part of the deal. I need to understand where it all comes from. How important the work is to the families. I'm really pleased we're going to be part of this process."

"Me, too," she said. Although, she wouldn't be. Not once everything was in place. This was it for her.

"I'm going up to Doi Suthep, to see the temple. I thought you might want to come with me."

She did. Not just to see the temple, although that was of major interest to her, but to spend some time with him. It was that whole inconvenient paradox of being in love with her best friend again. She wanted to avoid him, because she felt conflicted over the kiss. She wanted to be with him, confide in him, because she felt conflicted, too.

"I..."

"Are you avoiding me?" he asked, hands on his lean hips. "Well, I know you're avoiding me, but I guess I don't know why. Does this have to do with you leaving Roasted?"

"No!"

"Then what the hell is your problem?"

Hot, reckless anger flooded her. "My problem? Are you serious? You asked me to come here, and play fiancée, and I have. I don't have a problem."

"When you aren't avoiding me."

"I have done exactly what you asked me to do," she said. "I have played the part of charming, simpering fiancée, I've worn this ring on my finger, and you can't, for one second see why that might not be...something I want to do. And then you kiss me. Kiss me like...like you really are on your honeymoon, and you want to know what my problem is?"

He looped his arm around her waist and drew her to him, his eyes blazing. She braced herself against him, her palms flat on his bare chest. "I think I do know what your problem is. I think you're avoiding me because of the kiss. Because you're afraid it will happen again. Or because you want it to happen again."

She shook her head slightly. "N-no. I haven't even thought about it again."

"Liar." He dipped his head so that his lips hovered just above hers. "You want this."

She did. She really did. She wanted his lips on hers. His hands on her body. She wanted everything. "You arrogant bastard," she said, her voice trembling. "How dare you?"

"How dare I what? Say that you want it again? We both know you do."

His lips were so close to hers and it was tempting, so tempting, to angle her head so that they met. So that she could taste him again. Have a moment of stolen pleasure again.

"You do want it," he said again, his voice rough, strained.

"So?" she whispered.

"What?"

"So what if I do?" she said, finding strength in her voice. "What then, Zack? We'll kiss? Sleep together? And then what? Nothing. You and I both know there won't be anything after that. We'll just ruin what we do have."

He released his hold on her and took a step back, letting his hands fall to his sides. "Sorry."

"You've been apologizing to me a lot lately," she said, her voice trembling. "You don't need to do that."

He nodded. "I'm going to take a quick shower."

"Not going to the temple?"

He smiled ruefully. "Still am. And you can come if you want. Provided you've worked the tantrum out of your system."

"That was your tantrum, Parsons, not mine."

"Maybe." He tightened his jaw, his hands curling into fists. "Just tense I suppose. Coming with me or not?"

She hesitated. Because she did want to go, but things

weren't…easy with him at the moment. And the scariest thing was she wasn't sure she wanted them to be easy again. She was sort of liking this new, scary dynamic between them. The one that made him touch her like she did something to him. Like he was losing control.

"I'll be good. I promise," he added.

She laughed, a fake, tremulous sound. "I wasn't worried."

Zack wasn't the one who worried her. She hesitated because she wasn't sure she trusted *herself* to behave.

"I was," he said, turning away from her and walking back into the house. She watched him the whole way, the muscles on his back, the dent just above the waistline of his jeans, and his perfect, tight butt.

She let out a slow, shaky breath. Yeah, it was definitely herself she didn't trust.

The temple at Doi Suthep was crowded with tourists, spiritual pilgrims and locals. Clara and Zack walked up the redbrick staircase, the handrails fashioned into guardian dragons with slithering bodies and fierce faces.

They were silent for the three-hundred-step trek up to the temple, Clara keeping a safe distance between them, in spite of the crush of people all around them. She was mad at him.

And fair enough, he'd been a jerk earlier. That was sexual frustration. Sexual frustration combined with the desire to give in to the need to kiss her again. To do more than kiss her.

Damn.

He could still remember the first time he'd seen Clara. She was working behind the counter at a bakery, flour on her cheeks. She was cute. Not the kind of woman he was normally attracted to. But she'd fascinated him. Utterly and completely. It had turned out she'd made great cupcakes, too. And that she was smart and funny. That it felt good to be with her.

The emotional connection to her, when he'd been lacking a connection with anyone for years, had been shocking, instant, and had immediately found him shoving his attraction to her away.

A friendship with her was fine. Anything else…he didn't have room for it. Anything else would go beyond the boundaries he'd set for himself. And he needed his boundaries. His control. He valued it above everything else.

Just another reason he'd intended to marry Hannah. Marriage brought stability, a sort of controlled existence that attracted him. One woman in his bed, in his life.

And now that that had gone to hell, it seemed his feelings for Clara were headed in the same direction. He'd done with her, for seven years now, what he did with everything in his life. She had a place. She was his friend. She didn't move out of that place in his mind.

His body was suddenly thinking differently. He'd made a mistake. He'd allowed himself too much freedom. He'd indulged his desire to look at her body. To touch her soft skin when they'd gone swimming. And that night, he'd given in to the temptation to allow her to feature in his fantasies. To find release with her image in his mind.

He'd allowed himself to cross the line in his mind, and that was where control started. He knew better. Yet it was hard to regret. Because wanting her was such a tantalizing experience. Just feeling desire for her was a pleasure on its own.

Her sweet, short, sundress was not helping matters. Though, thankfully she'd had to purchase a pair of silk pants to wear beneath it before they could head up toward the temple.

Still, even with her legs covered, there was that bright, gorgeous smile that had been plastered on her face since they'd arrived. She was all breathy sighs and sounds of pleasure over the sights and sounds. It was the sweetest torture.

"Incredible," she breathed, her voice soft, sensual in a way. Enough to make his body ache.

"Yes," he agreed. Mostly, he was looking at her, and not the immense, gold-laden temple.

He forced himself to look away from Clara. To keep his focus on the gilded statues, the bright, fragrant offerings of flowers, fresh fruit and cakes left in front of the different alters that were placed throughout the courtyard. A large, dome-shaped building covered entirely in gold reflected the sun, the air bright, thick with smoke from burning incense.

Monks in bright orange robes wove through the crowds, talking, laughing, offering blessing.

It *was* incredible. And still nowhere near as interesting as the woman next to him.

"Have you been enjoying yourself here?" he asked.

"More or less," she said, looking at him from the corner of her eye, color creeping into her cheeks. Probably not the smartest question to ask. Why was he struggling with his words and actions? That never happened to him. Not anymore.

"The less would be me being a jerk and planting my lips on you, right?" Might as well go for honesty. Clara was the only person in his life who rated that. He didn't want to violate it.

She blew out a breath. "Um...mostly the being a jerk. You're a pretty good kisser, it turns out."

"So you didn't mind that?"

"Not as much as I should have." Her words escaped in a rush.

"Glad to know I'm not the only one," he said, forcing the words out.

"Not sure it helps anything." She walked ahead of him, straying beneath the overhang of a curled roof, her eyes on the murals painted on the walls of the temple.

"Maybe not." He leaned in, pretending to examine the same image she was.

"So...is there a solution?" She put her hand on the wall, tracing the painting of a white elephant with her finger.

He covered her hands with his, his heart pounding, his hand shaking like he was a teenage virgin. "Let me see."

He leaned in, his mouth brushing hers. He went slow this

time, asking the question, as he should have done the first time he'd kissed her. She didn't move, not into him or away from him. He angled his head and deepened the kiss and he felt her soften beneath him, her lips parting beneath his, her breath catching, sharp and sweet when the tip of his tongue met hers.

He pulled away, his eyes on hers.

She released a breath. "How do you feel?"

"I was going to ask you the same thing."

She looked up. "The roof didn't fall in."

"No," he said, following her gaze. "It didn't."

She leaned into him, her elbow jabbing his side, a shy smile on her face. "Good to know anyway."

"Glad it comforts you."

She laughed, her cheeks turning pink, betraying the fact that she wasn't unaffected. "Comfort may not be the right word."

He looked around the teeming common area, at the completely unfamiliar surroundings. And he found he wanted to pretend that the feelings he was having for Clara were unfamiliar, too.

But he couldn't. Because they had been there, for a long time, lurking beneath the surface. Ignored. Unwanted. But there.

"No. Comfort is definitely not the right word."

They'd spent most of the day at the temple, then taken a car back to Chiang Mai where they'd wandered the streets buying food from vendors, and watching decorations go up on every market stall for a festival that was happening in the evening.

Now, with the event coming close, the streets were packed tight with people, carrying street food, flower arrangements with candles in the center, talking, laughing. It was dark out, the sun long gone behind the mountains, but the air was still thick, warm and fragrant. There was music, noise and movement everywhere. The smell of frying food mixed with the perfume of flowers and the dry, stale scent of dust clung to the air, filled her senses.

It almost helped block out Zack. But not quite. No matter just how much it filled up her senses, it couldn't erase Zack. The imprint of his kiss. It had been different than the first one. Tender. Achingly sexy.

It had made her want more. Not simply in a sexual way, but in an emotional way. It didn't bear thinking about. Still, she knew she would.

She kept an eye on the food stalls, passing more exotic fare, like anything with six legs or more, for something a bit more vanilla. Maybe food would help keep her mind off things. At least temporarily.

"I definitely don't need this," she said, stopping to buy battered, fried bananas from the nearest food stall.

"But you bought it," he said, breaking a piece off the banana and putting it in his mouth.

"Well, that's because sweets are my area of expertise. You're here for the beans and tea leaves, I'm here for the pairing, right? This is research. It's for work. I need to capture the new and exotic flavor profiles Chiang Mai has to offer," she said, trying to sound official. "Maybe I can write off the calories?"

They dodged a bicycle deliveryman and crossed the busy, bustling street, moving away from the stalls and toward the river that ran through the city. "You don't need to worry about it. You're perfect like you are."

She looked down at the bag of sweets. "You're just saying that."

"I'm not."

She sucked in a sharp breath and looked at the lanterns that were strung from tree to tree, glowing overhead. "We should do this more. At home."

"Eat?"

"No. Go do things. Mostly we work, and sometimes I feed

you at my house, or we watch a movie at yours. Well, we do go
out to lunch sometimes, but on workdays, so it doesn't count."

"We're busy."

"We're workaholics."

Zack frowned and stopped walking. He extended his hand
and took a lock of her hair between his thumb and forefinger,
rubbing it idly. "Is that why you're leaving me?"

She looked up at him. "I'm not leaving you. I'm leaving the
company." And she was counting on that to put some natural
and healthy distance between them. Roasted had brought them
together, and because they got along so well, after spending the
day at work together, half of the time it felt natural to simply
go and have dinner together. Watch bad reality TV together.
Once they weren't involved in the same business it would only
be natural they would drift apart. And with any luck, it would
only feel like she was missing her right arm for a couple of
years.

"What do you need? I'll give it to you."

"You're missing the point, Zack. It's about having something of my own."

"Roasted isn't enough for you? You've been there from the
beginning, more or less. You've helped me make it what it is."

"No. I just bake cupcakes. And there are a lot of people who
can do my job."

"But they aren't you."

She closed her eyes and let the compliment wash over her.
She'd say this for Zack; he gave her more than most anyone
else in her life ever had, including her family. But it was still
just a crumb of what she wanted.

"No," she said, "some of them are even better."

She wove through the crowd to the edge of the waterfront.
People were kneeling down and putting the flower arrangements with their lit candles into the stream. The crowd standing on the other side of the waterfront was lighting candles

inside tall, rice paper lanterns, the orange spreading to the inky night, casting color and light all around.

Zack was behind her, she could sense it without even turning around. "I'm glad we came tonight," she said.

Zack swept his fingers through Clara's hair, moving it over her shoulder, exposing her neck. He didn't normally touch her like that, but tonight, he found he couldn't help himself. Things were tense between them. The kiss at the temple certainly hadn't helped diffuse it.

He wondered if most of the tension had started in the bedroom back in the villa. That moment when they'd both looked at the bed and had that same, illicit thought.

If it had started there, they might be able to finish it there.

Temptation, pure and strong, lit him on fire from the inside out. She turned, and his heart slammed hard against his rib cage, blood rushing south of his belt, every muscle tensing. He could feel the energy change between them, like a wire that had been connecting them, unseen and unfelt for years had suddenly come alive with high-voltage electricity. He knew she felt it, too.

"We broke things, didn't we?" she whispered.

It was like she read his thoughts, which, truly, was nothing new. But inconvenient now, since his thoughts had a lot to do with what it might be like to see her naked.

"Because of the kisses?"

She nodded once. "I can't forget them."

"I can't, either. I'm not sure if I want to."

She took a deep breath. "That's just what I was thinking earlier."

"Was it?"

"Yes. I should want to forget it, we both should. So we can get things back to where they're supposed to be but..."

He leaned down and pressed his lips to hers, soft again. "Do you think we could break it worse than we already have? Or is the damage done?"

"I have no idea."

Everything in him screamed to step back. Because this was an unknown. A move that would affect his life, his daily life, and he couldn't see the way it would end. And that just wasn't how he did things. Not since that night when he'd been sixteen and he'd acted unthinkingly, impulsively, and ruined everything.

He wasn't that person anymore. He'd made sure of it. If he didn't walk away from Clara now, from the temptation she presented, if he didn't plan it out and look at all the angles, he was opening them both up to potential fallout.

He stepped forward and kissed her again. Deepening the kiss this time, letting the blood that was roaring in his ears drown out conscious thought.

Clara knew she should stop this. Stop the madness before it went too far. It already had gone too far. It had gone too far the moment she agreed to come. Because the desire for this, for the week to turn into this, had been there. Of course, she'd never imagined that Zack would—could—want her.

The breaking of things wasn't just down to the kiss. It was the day at the river, the intense moment on the balcony. The fact that she'd realized she was deeply, madly, irrevocably in love with a man who was just supposed to be her friend.

He kissed the tip of her nose, then her cheeks. "Zack," she whispered.

"Clara."

"Are we trying to see if we can break things worse?"

"Actually, I'm not thinking at all. Not about anything beyond what I feel right now."

"What is it you feel?" she asked, echoing what she'd said after they'd kissed.

"I want you."

She hesitated, her heart squeezing tight. "Do you want me? Or do you want to have sex?"

He looked at her for a long time, the glow of flames across

the river reflected in his eyes. "I want you, Clara Davis. I have never slept with one woman when I wanted another one, and I would never start the practice with you. When I have you, I won't be thinking of anyone else. I'll only have room for you."

His words trickled through her, balm on her soul. Exactly the right words.

The real question was, did she want to accept a physical relationship when it was only part of what she wanted?

You only have part of what you want now. A very small part.

"Just for tonight," she said, hating that she had to say it, but knowing she did. Because she knew for certain that there could be no romantic future for them. She loved him, she was certain of it now. She had for a long time, possibly for most of the seven years she'd known him. It had been a slow thing, working its way into her system bit by bit. With every smile, every touch.

And he didn't love her. Looking at him now, the light in his eyes, that wasn't anything deeper than lust. But if that was all she could have, she would take that. Right now, she would take it, and she wouldn't think about the wisdom of it, or the consequences.

Because she was staring hard into a Zack-free future, and she would rather have all of him tonight, and carry the memory with her, than be nothing more than his trusty sidekick forever, standing by watching while he married another woman. Watching him make a life with someone else, someone he didn't even love, while her heart splintered into tiny pieces with every beat.

"One night," she repeated. "Here. Away from reality. Away from work and home. Because… We can't keep going on like this. It can't be healthy."

The people around them started cheering and she looked around them, saw the paper lanterns start to rise up above them, filling the air with thousands of floating, ethereal lights.

"Just one night," he said, his voice rough. "One night to explore this." He touched her cheek. "To satisfy us both. Is that really what you want?"

"I want you. So much."

He kissed her without preliminaries this time, her body pressed against hers, his erection thick and hard against her stomach as his mouth teased and tormented her in the most delicious way. She wrapped her arms around his neck and gave herself up to the heat coursing between them. When they parted she felt like she was floating up with the lanterns.

One night. The proposition made her heart ache, and pound faster. It excited her and terrified her. She didn't know what she was thinking. But one thing she did know: he wanted her. He wasn't faking the physical reaction she'd felt pressed against her.

The very thought of Zack, perfect, sexy Zack wanting her, was intoxicating. Empowering. She wanted to revel in the feeling. One night. To find out if her fantasies were all she'd built them up to be. One night to have the man of her dreams.

One night to make a memory that she would carry with her for the rest of her life.

CHAPTER SEVEN

BACK at the villa, Clara started to question some of the bravado she'd felt down in the city. It was one thing to know, for a moment, in public, fully dressed, that Zack was attracted to her. It was another to suddenly forget a lifetime's insecurity. To wonder if it would be Hannah on his mind.

They were in the bedroom. And her eyes were fixed on the bed, that invitation to decadence, to passion unlike anything she'd ever known. With the man she loved.

She sucked in a breath. She wasn't going to worry about how attracted he was to her, where she ranked with his other lovers. This night was for her. It was the culmination of every fantasy, every longing she'd had since Zack had walked into the bakery she worked at seven years ago and offered her a job.

He pulled her to him and kissed her. Hungry. Wild. She felt it, too, an uncontrollable, uncivilized need that had no place anywhere else in her life. No one had ever made her feel like this. No one had ever made her want to forget every convention, every rule, and just follow her body's most untamed needs.

But Zack did.

"I want you," she said, her voice breaking as they parted. She had to say it. Because it had been building in her for so long and now she felt like she was going to burst with it.

"I want you, too. I've thought of this before," Zack said, unbuttoning his shirt as he spoke, revealing that gorgeous, toned chest. "Of what it might be like to see you."

"To...to see me?"

"Naked," he said.

"You have?" she asked, her voice trembling now, because she'd hoped, maybe naively, that he would want the lights off. She didn't want him to see her. Touch, yes. Taste, sure. But see?

"Of course I have. I've tried not to think about it too hard. Because you work for me. Because you're my friend. And it's not good to picture friends or employees naked. In my life, everything has a place, and yours was never supposed to be in my bed. And I was never supposed to imagine you naked. But I have anyway sometimes."

"I have a hard time believing that."

"Why?" He shrugged his shirt off and let it fall to the floor, then his hands went to his belt and her breath stuck in her throat.

"Because I'm...average."

He chuckled, his hands freezing on the belt buckle. "Damn your mother for making you believe that garbage." He took a step toward her and put his hand on her cheek, his thumb sliding gently across her face. "You are exquisite. You have such perfect skin. Smooth. Soft. And your body." He put his other hand on her waist. "I thought of you last night. Of this. Of how beautiful you would look."

Reflexively she pulled back slightly.

"What?" he asked.

"I'm not... What was Hannah? A size two? I'm...I'm not a size two."

"Beauty isn't a size. I don't care what the number on the tag of your dresses says. I don't care what your sister looked like, or what your mother thought you should look like. I know what I see. You have the kind of curves other women envy."

He reached around and caught the tab on her summer dress with his thumb and forefinger and tugged it down partway.

Her hands shook, her body trembling inside and out. She felt like she was back beneath the spotlight again. Just waiting to have all of her flaws put out there for everyone to ridicule.

"Wait," she said.

His hands stilled. "I don't know if I can."

"Please. Can were turn the lights off?"

There was only one lamp on. It wasn't terribly bright in the room, but she still felt exposed already, with the zipper barely open across the top part of her back. She felt awkward. Unexceptional. Especially faced with all of Zack's perfection. He didn't have an ounce of spare flesh, every muscle perfectly defined as though he were carved from granite.

He put his hands on her hips and pulled her to him. She could feel his erection again, hard and hot against her. "You are perfect." He moved his hands around to her back, to her bottom, cupping her. She gasped. She'd never been this intimate with a man. She wondered if she should be more or less nervous that it was Zack she was finally taking the step with.

No one had seen her naked, not since she was in diapers. She didn't even change in public locker rooms. She would hide in bathroom stalls, needing the coverage of four walls and a door. And Zack wanted...

"Please."

"Let me see you first." Her eyes met his and she drew in an unsteady breath. "It's me, Clara."

"I know," she said.

"When you're ready."

She took a breath and turned away from him, catching the zipper and tugging it down the rest of the way, letting her dress fall to the floor. Zack moved behind her, his arm curving around her, his palm pressed flat against her stomach.

He swept her hair to the side and pressed a kiss to her neck. "As I said. Perfection."

He turned her slowly, keeping his arms around her, holding her against him, his hard body acting as a shield. Cocooned in his arms, she didn't feel quite so naked.

She looked at his eyes, so familiar, yet different at the same time. Zack's eyes, filled with a kind of raw lust she'd never had directed at her before. Not by him, not by any man. The enormity of the moment hit her then. She was about to be with Zack. About to make love to him.

She started shaking then, her hands, her entire body, from the inside out. He wrapped his arms around her and held her against him. "Are you okay?"

"Yes," she said, her voice shaking. "I'm okay."

"Why are you shaking?" She couldn't answer. "Be honest," he said.

"Because it's you."

He tilted his head to the side and kissed her. She closed her eyes determined to do nothing more than luxuriate in the moment. The heat of his mouth, the slide of his tongue. She was going to believe, in this moment, that she could be the woman he wanted.

He reached around and unhooked her bra. He pulled back from her for a moment so he could remove it the rest of the way, leaving her exposed to his hungry gaze. "I said you were perfection, but I didn't know just how true that was."

A hot flush spread over her entire body, heating her. Embarrassment battling with desire.

He cupped her breasts, sliding his thumbs over her nipples. And that was when desire won. She shook with pleasure, her stomach tightening, her internal muscles pulsing, her body ready, demanding, more of him. Demanding climax. She was close to finding it, with just the touch of his hands. Maybe it was because in her mind she had found pleasure with him so many times, in reality, it was effortless to get close to the peak.

A hoarse sound caught in her throat and she felt herself go over the edge. She gripped his forearms, her fingernails digging into his flesh. As soon as the numbing pleasure washed away, embarrassment crashed in on her. She couldn't believe she'd come so quickly. Telling in so many ways. She hadn't realized just how impossible it would be to keep secrets when they were like this, hadn't realized just how intimate it would be.

"I..." She looked at his face, and his expression stole the words from her lips. A look of pure masculine satisfaction, combined with total arousal. The embarrassment dissolved. She reached forward and put her hands on his belt buckle, undoing it and pulling his belt from the loops.

He pulled her to him again, kissing her like a starving man. She reached between them and undid the closure on his pants, pushing them down his hips, along with his underwear. She felt his bare flesh against her for the first time, so impossibly hot and hard.

She wrapped her fingers around him and squeezed. She wasn't sure why, only that she wanted to. That she wanted to touch him, taste him, everywhere. To make him feel half of what he'd made her feel.

So this would be about him, a little bit. But mostly, she was just going to enjoy having the man she'd dreamed of having for so long, completely available to her. For tonight, he was hers.

He put his hand on her thigh and pulled her leg up over his hip. She held on to his shoulders and he curled his fingers around her other thigh, lifting her off the ground and walking her to the bed, up the step, laying her down on the soft mattress, his body over hers, making her feel small. Feminine. Beautiful.

He dipped his head and slid the tip of his tongue around the edge of one of her nipples. She arched into him and he sucked the tip into his mouth, his eyes never leaving hers.

"You're so sensitive there," he said, his voice sounding different, strained. "I love it."

"I like it, too," she said. It was the first time she'd ever really liked her body.

He tugged her panties down her thighs and she helped kick them off of the bed. "I stand by what I said earlier. Perfection." He kissed her ribs, just beneath her breasts, down to her belly button. "Designed to take pleasure. For me to give you pleasure. Exquisite." He moved lower, his lips teasing the tender skin. He parted her thighs and slid his tongue over her clitoris. White heat shot through her body, a deep, intense pleasure tightening her muscles. She gripped the sheets, trying to hold herself to the bed.

He slid one finger inside her and she thought she might explode. Then another finger joined the first and a slight stinging sensation cut through the pleasure. She held her breath for a moment and waited for it to fade. It would. She knew it would. And all the better if he took care of it this way.

He worked his fingers in and out of her body, each time, the discomfort lessened. And he didn't seem to notice. Which was fine by her.

"I can't wait anymore," he said, his voice rough, broken.

"I don't think I can wait, either."

He moved up so that the head of his erection was testing the entrance to her body, his arms bracketing hers, his biceps trembling slightly. He was as undone as she was. It was such a wonderful, incredible feeling. It made her truly believe that she was beautiful.

He pushed into her partway then pulled out completely, swearing sharply.

"What?" she asked, hoping it had nothing to do with her virginity. Because she couldn't stop. Not now.

"Condoms," he said, his hands unsteady as he opened the drawer to the bedside table. He opened the box and pulled out a packet, getting the condom out and rolling it on to his length quickly.

"Oh. Good." She didn't know why she hadn't thought of

it. She should have. But there were so many things filling her head. So many emotions. She'd almost forgotten the most important thing.

Then he was back, poised over her, ready to enter her.

He slid back in as far as he'd already been, then pressed in the rest of the way. It was tight, but it wasn't painful, the evidence of her virginity likely dealt with earlier.

He flexed his hips, his pelvis pressing against her clitoris at exactly the right angle, the sensation of him being inside her as her muscles clenched tight around him so incredible she couldn't stop the moan of pleasure from escaping her lips.

She gripped his tight, muscular butt, so much more perfect than she'd even imagined. Everything so much more perfect than she'd imagined.

She wrapped her legs around his calves and held him to her, moving in rhythm with his thrusts, the pleasure building low in her stomach, emotion swelling in her chest, threatening to overflow. It came to a head, pushing her until she was certain that unless she found release, she would break apart into tiny little pieces beneath the weight of the pressure inside of her.

Then she was falling apart, splintering, release, pleasure, love, pouring through the cracks, filling her, washing through her. She dug her fingernails into his back, squeezing her eyes closed tight. She didn't even try to stop the sharp cry that was climbing her throat, couldn't feel embarrassed that she was arching and moving against him with no control at all.

Because he was right with her, his entire body trembling, his fist gripping the comforter by her head, a low, intense growl rumbling in his chest as he found his own release.

He lay above her, his breathing harsh, his heart pounding so hard she could hear it. And she was pretty sure he could hear hers, too.

"Wow," she said.

He moved to the side, withdrawing from her body, one arm resting on her body. He was watching her closely, like he wanted to ask her something. Or like he thought he should but didn't want to.

"You've never been careful about what you said to me before," she said. "Don't start now."

He huffed a laugh. "Clara…"

"Actually I changed my mind," she said. "We have one night. Why talk about anything?"

Something in his expression changed, hardened. "I think that's a good idea." He rolled to his side and stood up. "I'll be back in a minute."

He went into the bathroom and came back out a moment later.

"What do you propose we do, if we aren't going to talk?"

She got up on her knees and went to the edge of the bed, wrapping her arms around his neck, uncharacteristic boldness surging through her. "I'm sure we can think of a few things."

This was her night to have all of the man she loved. And she wasn't going to miss out on a single experience.

Morning came too quickly, light breaking through the gauzy curtain that surrounded the bed, bringing reality in with the sunbeams.

She didn't want the night to end. She didn't want to face reality. She'd felt like a princess last night; beautiful, desired. She'd felt like her dream was in her grasp. And this morning she felt like she'd turned back into a pumpkin. Reality sucked.

She looked at the man sleeping next to her, the only man she'd ever really wanted. The only man she'd ever loved.

And today, she would have to get up and forget that last night had happened. She would have to consign it to the "perfect memories" bin along with other things she pulled out when she was feeling lonely, or when things weren't going well.

The thought made her whole body hurt.

"I arranged to have the plane leave in an hour or so," he said, his eyes still closed.

"Okay," she said, swallowing thickly and sliding out of the bed, clutching the sheet tightly to her breasts, desperate to cover herself now, in the light of day. It was one thing to feel sexy, to be all right with her nudity when he was looking at her like he was starving and she was a delicacy. A lot less easy when he seemed...uninterested.

"I'm going to take a shower real quick."

He made a noise that might have been a form of consent, but she didn't ask for confirmation before beating a hasty retreat to the bathroom. She turned the water on and sat on the closed toilet lid, letting the tears fall down her cheeks, hoping the sound of the water hitting the tile would drown out the sound of her sobs.

Zack sat up, a curse on his lips. Last night...last night had been an aberration. A hot, amazing aberration, maybe, but it could never happen again. He had been careless. He'd nearly forgotten to use a condom. And she'd been a virgin.

If he'd thought about it, if he'd thought at all, he would have guessed that. He knew her well enough to have picked up on how nervous she was, to understand what that meant. He also knew her well enough to know she wasn't really a one-night-stand woman. She was sensitive, emotional. Sweet.

His stomach twisted, nausea overtaking him, spreading through his limbs. She probably wasn't on birth control, and there was a possibility that in that moment, when he'd been inside of her without protection, that he'd made a very big mistake.

No, he knew he'd made a mistake. He hit his fist on the top of the nightstand and stood, stalking through the room collecting his clothes. Had he learned nothing? Was he as stupid now as he'd been fourteen years ago?

His heart froze for a moment, the events of what sometimes felt like a past life, playing through his head from start to finish. Like a horror film he couldn't pause.

No. He'd worked way too hard to leave that person behind. That boy, who had been so irresponsible. Who had caused so much damage.

Last night he'd lost control. With Clara, of all people. She shouldn't have tempted him like that. But she had. She'd made him shake like *he* was the virgin.

It couldn't happen again. It wouldn't. He might have lost his control for a moment, but he wouldn't do it again.

Clara appeared a few moments later, her face scrubbed fresh and pink, her hair wet and wavy. She was dressed, a fitted T-shirt and jeans meaningless now since he'd already seen her naked and his mind was doing a very good job of envisioning her as she'd been last night.

All pale skin and soft curves. Pure perfection. Better than he'd ever imagined.

"Hey," she said, trying to smile and not quite managing it.

"Are you all right?" he asked. He'd never slept with a virgin before, but that was only part of the foreign, first-time feeling he was dealing with. The other part of that was because it was Clara. And the rest was because of his carelessness.

Carelessness that had to be addressed.

"I'm fine," she said.

"Are you on birth control?" he asked.

She narrowed her eyes. "No."

He tried to get a handle on the gnawing panic in his gut. Condoms were reliable. He knew that. But there was the matter of his impatience, of his entering her, even briefly, without protection. He swore. "Why not?"

"What?" She crossed her arms beneath her breasts. "I'm sorry, was I supposed to start taking the pill just in case you invited me on your honeymoon and we hooked up? I was a virgin, you jackass."

"I know," he shouted, not sure why he was shouting, only that his blood was pumping too fast through his veins and his heart was threatening to thunder out of his chest. "I know," he said again, softer this time.

"You used a condom," she said, her cheeks flushing pink.

"Yes, I did, eventually. There's a chance that kind of carelessness could have gotten you pregnant. It's not a big chance, but there is a chance."

"I…I seriously doubt that I'm pregnant. Well, obviously I'm not pregnant yet since things take a while to travel and…well, that's high-school health, you know all that."

"But there's a chance. I'm usually more careful."

"Zack, I think you're overreacting."

"Is that what you think, Clara?" he asked, his voice deadly calm. "You think I'm overreacting because you think it can't happen. But then, you've never been pregnant, obviously. And I have gotten a woman pregnant, so I think I might be a bit more in touch with that reality than you are. Do you know what it's like? To know that everything in your life is going to have to change because for one moment you were so utterly selfish and consumed with one moment of pleasure that you didn't think about anything else?"

Clara's heart was in her throat. She felt like she couldn't breathe. It was like a shield had been torn away from Zack, like his armor had dissolved, crumbled around his feet, leaving nothing but the man he was beneath his facade. A facade she hadn't realized was there.

This was the man she'd seen glimpses of. The reason for the darkness that she saw in his eyes sometimes. And she was afraid to hear the rest. But she had to.

His chest rose and fell sharply. "I was sixteen. And I was more interested in getting some than thinking about using a condom. Turns out you can get someone pregnant after just one time, regardless of the idiot rumors floating around the high school saying otherwise."

She didn't ask him what happened. She didn't interrupt the break. She just let his silence fill the room, and she felt his pain. Felt it in her, through her. She didn't have to know what happened to know that it was bad. Devastating. To know that knowing it was going to change her. The way it had changed Zack.

"I didn't want a baby, but we were having one. She wanted it. I didn't want him," he said. "But I got a job so that I could pay for the doctor bills. So I could help her raise him. Because at least I knew that I should do the right thing." A muscle in his jaw jerked. "He came too early. And by the time I realized how badly I did want him, it was too late. By the time I realized that a baby can very quickly mean everything in the world to you, he was gone."

She tried to hold back the sob that was rising inside her. His face was blank now, void of emotion, flat. Like he was reading a story in a newspaper, not telling her about his life.

"Another reason Hannah was so perfect for me," he said. "She didn't want kids."

"You don't... You don't want kids?"

"I had one, Clara. I would never...I will never put myself through something like that again. I nearly died with him. I don't make the same mistakes twice. I'm always careful now."

Except last night, he wasn't as careful as he usually was, obviously. And she wasn't sure how she felt about that. Or what it might mean. And right now, she wished they had never slept together. Because she wanted to comfort him as a friend. To tell him how much her heart ached for him. But she wasn't sure if it was her place now. She wasn't sure what she was supposed to do. What he expected. What he would allow.

Because now she saw just how much he had always hidden from her. She saw a stranger. She wondered if it was even possible that this man, hard and angry, was the same man she'd seen every day for the past seven years.

"How did you...how did you cope with it?"

"I don't need to talk about it, Clara. I don't talk about it, ever. This isn't an invitation for you to psychoanalyze me. But now you know why I insist on being careful. That's the important part of the story. And you'll tell me, if you're pregnant."

"I'll let you know," she said. "But I'm sure everything will be fine."

He turned away from her and shrugged his shirt on.

"Everything will be fine," she repeated. That assurance was just for her. And she wasn't certain she believed it.

CHAPTER EIGHT

THE plane ride back to San Francisco was a study in torture. Zack was hardly speaking to her and she felt battered from the inside out. Her body was a little bit sore from her first time, and her heart felt like it had been wrung out and left to dry.

Zack was acting overly composed. His focus on work, not on her. Not on the revelation that had passed between them, both in bed and out.

She didn't feel like the same person. She felt changed. She wasn't sure if Zack was the same person, either. Or maybe he was; maybe it was just that she saw him better now.

"I think I'll probably take a couple days off," she said, looking over at Zack who was engrossed in his laptop screen. "Recover. From the jet lag."

"Fine."

The chill in his response made her shiver. "And I'm thinking of buying a pony."

"You don't have anywhere to keep one," he said drily, still not looking up.

"Just a small one. For the rooftop garden."

He did look up this time. "Your neighbors would complain."

"I don't like my neighbors." That earned her a slight smile. "So, what's the plan when we get back to civilization?"

"With any luck, things can go back to normal."

Two questions flitted through her mind. Luck for who? And, what's normal? She didn't voice either of them. "Okay."

"I still need you there, at Roasted, until Amudee signs off on the deal."

"Right." She looked down at her hand. The ring was still there. "You'll want this back, I assume." She pulled the ring off and got up, walking over to his seat and depositing it on the desk in front of him. "Since we won't need it."

A relief. Wearing another woman's ring made her feel weighted down.

"No. We won't." His eyes met hers and held. She felt heat prickle down her arms, her nipples tightening as a flash of arousal hit her.

"Great. I'll um…I'm going to try to sleep."

As she drifted off in the plane's bedroom, she tried not to be disappointed that Zack didn't join her.

"Amudee is coming here."

Clara looked up and saw Zack. For the first time since they'd landed in San Francisco three days earlier. She'd taken a couple of days to get over her jet lag, and had sneaked around the office yesterday like a cat burglar, trying to get work done without encountering him.

Because ultimately, avoiding him was simply easier than trying to juggle all the emotions she felt when she saw him. Cowardly? Yes, yes, it was. But she felt a bit yellow-bellied after all that had happened between them, and she was wallowing in it.

"What?"

"He's coming here to see how we run our operation. He wants to talk to employees, to see where we work. If we truly do conduct business in an ethical manner."

Zack reached into his pocket and took out an overly familiar velvet box. He set it on the edge of her desk, his expression grim. "And now it continues. And every single person working in the this office has to believe it, too."

"Zack this can't... It has to end."

"It will. After. And you can take as much money as you need for a start-up. You can have my blessing, hell, you can have free Roasted coffee for the first five years. But I want this deal to go through."

"Ironic that you're trying to convince him of your business ethics by using a lie," she said, annoyance spiking inside her.

"Odd that it's necessary, too, don't you think?"

"He's a nice man."

"And a romantic, it seems. He loves you. He wants to make sure he sees us together as a couple again while he's here."

"Tangled web," she snapped, putting her pencil down on the desk.

"Isn't it?"

The air between them seemed to crackle, everything slowing for a moment, the silence so tense and brittle she was certain she could splinter it into tiny pieces if she spoke.

"Put it on," he said, looking at the ring.

"I gave it back," she said tightly.

"Clara, I need you to do this for me."

She fought the urge to make a rude gesture with a different finger than the one meant for a ring and grabbed the box, opened the lid and slid the ring on. "There."

"Come on."

"What?"

"We have to make an announcement."

"Zack..."

"We're going to see this through, right? Then you can leave. Whatever you need to do, you can go do it, but finish this with me."

"Fine." She stood up and rounded the desk, he wrapped his arm around her waist and drew her to him. Heat exploded in

her, stronger than she remembered, more arousing than anything had a right to be.

Instantly she was assaulted by images of their night together.
His mouth, his hands, the way it had felt when he was over her,
in her. It was torture. She clenched her hands into fists and the
heavy ring band bit into her fingers.

There was a small group of employees who worked on her
floor, their desks clustered in the center of the room. Roasted's
office had a social atmosphere, which Zack had always believed
made for optimum creativity. Because Zack was a great boss,
the kind who made everyone feel appreciated, all the time.

And he never, ever showed the dark, tortured side of himself she'd seen in Chiang Mai. He never showed the intense,
sexual side of himself, either. But she'd seen it. She'd felt it.

"Clara and I have an announcement to make."

Ten heads instantly popped up, eyes trained on her and
Zack. Her heart started pounding, her palms sweating. It was
one thing to lie to a man she'd never met before. A thing she
hated. But it was really quite another to lie to people she worked
with every day. People who she considered her friends.

"We're getting married," he said.

"Pay up." Cynthia, a woman with gray hair and pronounced
smile lines turned to Jess, a twenty-something computer whiz
who did their online marketing.

Jess swore and took his wallet out.

"What is this?" Clara asked.

"Congratulations," Cynthia said, beaming. "We had bets
placed on this. I bet you would get married. Most everyone
changed sides when Mr. Parsons got engaged to someone else.
But I held out. And now I'm collecting."

"Unbelievable," Clara muttered. She wasn't sure how she
felt about this revelation, either. A little bit flattered that people believed it was possible.

"Clearly I'm not giving people enough work to do," Zack said.

"Kiss her!" This from Jess, who undoubtedly considered it a consolation prize.

Everything inside Clara seized up, her muscles locking tight. Zack looked down at her, his fingers brushing her jaw. He dipped his head and kissed her. A perfectly appropriate kiss to give her in front of his employees. Nothing scandalous or overly sexual. But it grabbed hold of her world and shook it completely. Shook her.

When he lifted his head there was a smattering of applause. "Feel free to spread the news," Zack said, lacing his fingers through hers and leading her toward his office.

He closed the door tightly behind him, taking long strides to the far window that overlooked the bay, his back turned to her.

"Good show," she said icily.

He looked over his shoulder. "You could have been a little less stiff," he said.

"You..." She strode across the room, embracing the anger, unrest and desire that was rioting through her. "You..." She grabbed the lapels of his jacket and stretched up onto her toes, kissing him with every last ounce of passion and frustration that she felt.

He locked his arm around her waist and drew her up tight against his body, his erection hard and hot against her. He spun them around and backed her against the wall, pressing her against the hard surface, his lips hungry as he tasted her, feasted on her.

She wrapped her arms around him, sifted her fingers through his thick brown hair, holding him to her as she returned each stroke and thrust of his tongue. The days of not touching him, thinking of him and denying herself the pleasure of even seeing in him, crashed in on her, fueled her desperation.

She growled in frustration, needing more, faster. Now. She pushed his jacket down his arms and onto the floor, grabbing the knot on his tie and tugging it down as he put his hands on her thighs and pushed the hem of her skirt up. She wrapped one leg around his calf and arched against him.

He tore his mouth away from hers and put his palm flat on the wall behind them, a short, sharp curse punctuated by heavy breaths escaped his lips.

The full horror of what she'd done hit her all at once, like getting a bucket of freezing water dumped in her face. She echoed his choice of swear word and ducked beneath his arm, leaning forward and bracing herself on his desk.

"That shouldn't have happened," she said.

"For more than one reason."

"Why don't you list them?" she said sharply.

"Fine. I'll list them. We said one night. And that kind of kiss doesn't stop at just a kiss. The second reason is that you mean more to me than this," he said.

"Than what?"

"Than an angry make out session against a wall. Than you sneaking around, avoiding me, because we slept together. You mean more to me than sex."

That cut. And maybe it shouldn't have, but she couldn't separate having sex with Zack from the emotions she felt for him. She loved him; sex had been an expression of that. Being joined to him, intimate with him, it had been everything.

But not to him. To him, the sex was separate from the feeling.

"Great. But I apparently don't mean so much to you that you won't use me as a pretend fiancée." Her argument was thin, because frankly, if her feelings for him were platonic, the engagement thing would be nothing big at all.

But her feelings weren't platonic. Not even close.

"Then leave, Clara. If you don't want to do it, don't do it. I'm not holding you hostage. But understand this. I will likely lose the deal with Amudee, and then I won't be able to get the product I need to start the boutique stores. And my search for an acceptable product will continue. It will cost everyone time and money, lots of it. That's just stating a fact—it's not emotional blackmail or anything else you might be tempted to accuse me of."

Clara looked at his face, at the familiar planes and angles. The mouth she'd seen smile so many times, the lips she'd kissed just now. She knew him differently now than she had a week ago. She knew his body, she knew his loss. And as hard as it would have been for her to walk away then, it was impossible now. Impossible to leave him when she'd promised she would see this through.

"I'll do it. I'll play the part, I'll keep playing the part, I mean. But I didn't expect for it to go this far."

"I know. But we had a deal." He probably thought she meant the farce, but she was thinking of the sex. Or maybe he knew what she was really talking about and he was content to leave it ambiguous, just like she was.

"When the ink is dry on the agreement, it can be finished. You gave me your word," he said.

"That's low, Zack," she said, sucking in a deep breath, trying to make her lungs expand.

"It's true. I've been there for you when you needed me. I held your hair while you…"

"I know. Food poisoning. Please don't bring that up." It was right up there with her high-school humiliation. Zack watching her vomit. But he had taken care of her. There hadn't been anyone else. Truly, they were the key players in each other's lives. They were there for each other, at work and at home.

"My point is, I've helped you. Help me. I'm asking you as a friend, not your boss. Your friend."

She gritted her teeth, raw emotion, so intense she couldn't identify it, flooded her. She swung her arms back and forth, trying to ease the nervous energy surging through her limbs. "So when does Mr. Amudee get here?"

"Soon. He'll be in the office tomorrow morning, so it would be good if we came in together."

If they spent the night with each other, it would be even easier for them to commute to Roasted together, but she didn't say that. And she wouldn't. One night, that was all it was supposed to be and that was all it would be. Make-out sessions against the wall would be immediately stricken from record and forgotten. Completely.

"Then I'll see you tomorrow."

"We should probably leave together, too," he said.

"Probably." That would mean an evening waiting around for him to leave. "I'm going to go down to the kitchens and fiddle around with some recipes."

"I'll see you down there."

"See you then." Hopefully a little baking therapy would clear her mind. Because if not, they were both in trouble.

By the time Zack made it down to the kitchen he didn't have a handle on his libido or his temper. He'd figured a couple of hours separation for him and Clara would be a good idea, but it hadn't accomplished anything on his end.

No, he wouldn't feel satisfied until he was in bed with her again. Or just against the wall. That was why he had stopped kissing her, though. He didn't have a condom.

As an adult he hadn't had all that many lovers, mostly because he believed in taking things slowly, and making sure everything was completely safe. He liked for the woman to be on the pill, and he still used condoms, every time.

Already with Clara he'd been lax, skipping steps he hadn't since high school, and then he'd been ready to forgo any sort of protection in his office so that he could be with her again. In her. Because the truth of the matter was, he hadn't stopped thinking about how amazing that night had been since they'd arrived back in California. Not even close.

He'd dreamed of it, or rather, fantasized about it since sleep had eluded him. And when he hadn't been thinking about making love with her, he'd been replaying the moment he'd told her about his son. Over and over again.

He never talked about Jake. Ever. Not since he'd died, still in the hospital he'd never had a chance to leave, only a couple of days old. Sarah had never wanted to talk about it, and they hadn't had a romantic relationship at that point, anyway.

His parents…they had been horrified that their star football-playing son was going to give it all up to raise a child. If anything, they'd been relieved.

That day had changed everything. He'd been nothing more than a spoiled brat. An only child, destined to skate through college on a football scholarship. He'd taken everything, the adoration of the girls at his school, the free passes the teachers had given him, as his due.

But when Jake was born, he'd felt the weight of purpose. And when he died, it hadn't gone away. He hadn't fit anymore. In one blinding, clear moment he saw everything he'd done that was wrong, selfish, careless. He saw how his stupidity had cost everyone so much.

And he'd left. Left who he was. Left everyone he knew. And every day that passed was one day farther away from that awful day in the hospital. That day that had felt like someone reaching into his chest and yanking his emotions out, twisting them, distorting them.

He had never wanted to feel that way again. Ever. Even more importantly, he'd never wanted to have anything unplanned happen ever again. He wanted control. To plan, to consider the cost of his actions. To be in charge of his life.

He wasn't sure why he'd told Clara about it. Although she had asked why the birth-control lapse was such a big deal to him. But then, a few of his girlfriends had wanted to know why he used every method he could think of to prevent pregnancy. It had cost him relationships since the women involved had taken it as a sign of just how much he didn't want to be with them.

And while it was true he hadn't been looking for forever, his reasoning hadn't quite been what they'd assumed. Still, he hadn't felt compelled to tell them the story. Maybe it was because Clara was…Clara. She was the one person who had been in his life with any regularity for the past decade.

And now he'd likely screwed it up by sleeping with her. Or by kissing her. Or maybe he'd screwed it up the moment he'd asked her to play fiancée and go on his honeymoon.

He pushed open the stainless-steel double doors that led to the baking facility and saw Clara, bending down and looking in one of the ovens.

He took the opportunity to enjoy the view, the way her skirt hugged the round curve of her butt. It was a crime that she'd been made to feel insecure about those curves. He flashed back to the heady moments in his office, when he'd had her skirt pushed up around her hips, when he'd been ready to…

She straightened and turned, her brown eyes widening. "Oh! I didn't know you were here."

"Just walked in. What did you make me?"

"I think you'll like them. I have some cooling. I'm going to pass them out at lunch hour tomorrow."

"No walnuts?"

"None. They're Orange Cream. Don't look at me like that, they'll be good." She handed him a vaguely orange cupcake with white frosting, coated in bright orange sugar crystals.

"It has orange zest in the cake, and there's a Bavarian cream in the center. And the frosting is buttercream."

"All things I like." He took a bite, relishing the burst of sweet citrus and cream. She really was a genius. She'd hooked him with her cupcake-making skills the first time he'd met her, and he'd known then he had to have her for his company. That with her, his line of baked goods would be a massive success. And they had been.

And now she was leaving him.

"Good," he said, even though now he was having a hard time swallowing the bite.

"See? I told you."

"And I told you you wouldn't be easily replaced. You're the best at what you do."

She smiled, a sort of funny smile that almost made her look sad. "I do bake a mean cupcake. I'm glad you like them."

He wasn't going to ask her what was wrong. Because he wasn't sure if he could fix it, and he was afraid he might be the cause of it. "Ready to go?"

"Yes, ready. Oh, wait." She stopped and moved toward him, her eyes fixed on his mouth. His entire body was hot and hard instantly. Ready for her touch, her kiss. She extended her hand and put her thumb on the corner of his mouth. "You had some frosting there," she said, her tone as sweet as her cupcakes, her eyes filled with a knowing, sexual expression that told him she was tormenting him, and she knew it. It was going to be an interesting few weeks.

CHAPTER NINE

"I'm not going to bite you."

Clara glared at Zack from her position in the passenger side of his sporty little two-seater. She was clinging to the door handle, her shoulder smashed against the window. As much space between them as was humanly possible in the tiny metal cage.

The first words that bubbled up were *well that's a shame.* But she held them back, because she was not going to flirt with him. Was not. And she was going to forget about that lapse in the kitchen when she'd wiped the frosting from his mouth. She hadn't licked it off and that had been her first inclination, so really, her self-control was pretty rock solid.

"I know," she said. Much more innocuous than an invitation to bite her, that was for sure.

"Then stop clinging to the door handle like you're planning on jumping out when there's a lull in traffic."

She laughed, somehow, even though most of her felt anything but amused by the entire situation. "I'm not, I promise." She relaxed her hold on the door.

"Good." They pulled down into the underground parking lot of Roasted and into the spot that was second closest to the elevator. He'd given her the closest spot years ago. Some sort of chivalrous gesture, silly, but at the time she'd loved it.

He put the car in Park and killed the engine, getting out

and closing the door behind him. She watched him straighten his shirt collar through the window. He hated ties. He didn't wear them unless he had to. It was sexier when he didn't, in her opinion. It showed a little bit of his sculpted chest, a bit of dark hair. Of course, it was sexier when he didn't wear a shirt at all.

She felt the door give behind her and she squeaked, tightening her hold on the handle. Zack had opened it, just a bit, and was looking down at her, the expression on his face wicked.

"Are you going to sit in there all day? Because we have a meeting," he said.

"Creep," she said, no venom in her tone.

He winked and darn it all, it made her stomach turn over. "Only during business hours."

She released her hold on the door and he opened it the rest of the way, waiting for her to get out before pushing the up button on the lift. When they got in and the door closed, the easy moment evaporated.

The tension was back, and so thick she could hardly breathe. Judging by the sharp pitch of his chest when he drew in a breath, he felt the same. It made her feel better. Slightly.

"So, when is he coming in?"

"Soon," Zack said, his eyes fixed on the doors.

"Oh."

The elevator stopped and the doors slid open. Clara nearly sagged with relief as she scurried out of the elevator, eager to get back into non-shared air space.

When she and Zack walked into the main reception area the employees milling around, scavenging on last night's baking efforts stopped and clapped for them. She ducked her head and offered a smile and finger wave. She didn't know if Zack made a reciprocal gesture or not. She was far too busy not dying of humiliation.

The gleaming, golden elevator doors that would take them

up to their offices were just up ahead. She made a dash for it, and Zack got in behind her, the doors sliding closed.

"So many elevators," she said.

"Is that a problem?"

"Not at all," she said.

Two interminable minutes later they were on the floor that housed both of their offices. "I have work to do," she said, heading toward her own office. A little sanctuary would not go amiss.

"No time, Amudee is in the building. My office."

He put his hand on the small of her back and directed her into his office, closing the door behind them. A horrible, hot, tantalizing sense of déjà vu hit her. Their eyes clashed and held, his all steel heat and temptation. He took a step toward her just as the intercom on his desk phone went on.

"Mr. Parsons? Mr. Amudee is here to see you."

Zack leaned back and punched a button on the phone. "Send him in."

She wished she were relieved. She wasn't. She was just disappointed that she hadn't gotten to experience the conclusion of Zack's step forward. Of what he might have intended to do.

Zack's office door opened and the reason for their charade walked in, looking as personable and cheerful as ever, the lines by his dark eyes deepening as he smiled. "Good to see you again. Zack, I stopped by one of your locations here in the city on my way in, I was very impressed."

"Thank you, Mr. Amudee," Zack said, his charm turned on and dialed up several notches.

She watched Zack work, a sense of awe overtaking her. He was good, and she knew that, but seeing him in action was always incredible. He was smart and he was savvy. And the best part was, he really was a man of ethical business practices.

That, she knew, was the thing that made working with Amudee so important to him. Because he didn't just want to import coffee and tea from any farm. He didn't want to get involved in a share-cropping situation. He didn't want anyone being taken advantage of so that he could turn a profit.

Unfortunately Amudee seemed just as picky about who he did business with. And when money wasn't the be all and end all…you couldn't just throw dollars at it to solve everything. Dollars Zack had. It was the fiancée he'd found himself short of.

She toyed with the ring on her finger, her secondhand ring. The one that had belonged to Hannah. She would be a happy woman the moment she could get it off her finger and keep it off, that was for sure.

"So, dinner tonight, then?" Zack said. "Clara?" he prompted.

"Oh, yes. Tonight. Dinner."

"And as for today, I'd be happy to give you a tour of the corporate office. You can see how we run things here."

Mr. Amudee nodded in approval and started to head out the office door with Zack. "So," she said, "I think I'll go to my office and get some work done then."

"Great." He leaned in and kissed her cheek before walking out of the room.

She knew it was an empty gesture, all part of the show. But it still made her feel like she was floating to her office instead of walking. And no matter how much she tried to tell herself not to think about it, her cheek burned for the rest of the morning.

"What is this?"

When Zack had seen Clara's number flash onto his cell-phone screen, he'd heard her sweet hello before he'd even answered. So being greeted by a venomous hiss was an unexpected, unpleasant surprise.

"What is what, Clara? I'm currently battling traffic on North Point so I have no idea what you're talking about."

"This dress. This… Do you even call it a dress? I mean it's

short and slinky and I think the neckline is designed to show skin all the way down to a woman's belly button."

"I saw it, and I liked it, so I had my PA send it over."

"I agreed to a lot when I agreed to play fiancée, but I did not," she growled and paused for a moment before continuing, "agree to stuff myself into a gown that has all the give of saran wrap like a Vienna sausage!"

"I like the visual, but your attitude needs work."

"Your head needs work," she shot back.

"Wear the dress." He hung up the phone and tossed it onto the passenger seat before maneuvering his car against the curb in front of Clara's apartment.

He didn't bother to wait for the elevator. He took the stairs two at a time and knocked on her door, beneath the pretty, pink flowery wreath thing she had hung there. A clever ruse to make people think the owner of the apartment was sweetness and light when, at the moment, she was spitting flame and sulfur.

The door jerked open and he met Clara's glittering brown eyes. And then he looked down and all of the blood in his body roared south.

She was right about the dress. A deep scarlet, it would draw the eye of everyone in the restaurant. And while it didn't show her belly button, it did put her amazing cleavage on display. The soft, rounded curves of her breasts were accentuated by the sweetheart neckline, the pleating in the waist showing off just how tiny she was, before her hips flared out, the fabric conforming to that gorgeous, hourglass shape of hers.

"I am not going out in this."

"It's too late for you to change," he said, barely able to force himself to raise his eyes to her face. He had to admit, the dress was counterproductive as when it came to trying to put Clara back into the proper compartment she was meant to be in in his life, he didn't want her to change.

He wanted to look at her in that dress for as long as he could.

And then, he wanted to lower the zipper on the back of it and watch it slither down her body. He wanted to see her again, soft, naked and begging him to take her.

"Zack…"

"Do you have something against looking sexy?"

"What? No."

"Then what's the problem? If it honestly offends your modesty in some way, fine, change. But otherwise, you look…"

"Like I'm trying too hard?"

He took a step and she backed away from the door, letting him into the apartment. He shouldn't touch her. Not even an innocent gesture. Because with the thoughts that were running through his brain, nothing could be innocent.

He did anyway, and he ignored the voice in his head telling him to stay in control. He was in control. He could touch her without doing more. He was the master of his body, of his emotions.

He put his finger on her jaw, traced the line of it down her neck, to her exposed collarbone.

"You look effortless. As though bringing men to their knees is something you do every day of the week without breaking a sweat. You look like the kind of woman who can have anyone or anything she wants."

"I…I…well, I don't appreciate you dressing me," she said. "It's demeaning."

"I don't know if it was demeaning, but selfish, perhaps."

"Selfish?"

"Because I'm enjoying looking at you so much."

She bent down and picked up a black shawl from the couch, looping it over her arms before grabbing a black clutch purse from the little side table. "You shouldn't say things like that."

She breezed out the door ahead of him, clearly resigned to wearing the dress.

"Probably not," he said, his tone light.

"But you did anyway," she said, turning to face him.

"I did. There are a lot of things I shouldn't have said or done over the past couple of weeks, and yet, it seems I've said and done them all."

"I haven't," she said, turning away from him again and heading down the stairs, eager to avoid being in an elevator with him, he imagined.

"Oh, really?"

"Mmm. I have been virtuous. I've wanted to say and do many things in the past week that I haven't."

"Why do I feel disappointed by that news?"

"I don't know. You shouldn't be," she said, her stilettos clicking and echoing in the stairwell. "You should be thankful." She pushed open the exterior door and they both walked out into the cool evening air.

"I find I'm not."

"I can't help you there."

Something hot and reckless sparked in him. She must have noticed because she backed away from him until she bumped against his car. That was a picture, Clara, in scarlet silk, leaning against his black sports car. The fantasies that were rolling through his mind should be illegal.

"I wish you could," he said, taking a step toward her.

She shook her head. "There's no help for either of us."

"I'm starting to think that might be true."

He wanted to kiss the red off her lips. He wanted to take her back upstairs and do something about the unbearable ache that had settled in his body more than a week ago and hadn't released him since.

"Let's go. We have a dinner date," he said, his voice curt, harsher than he'd intended.

She nodded and went around to the passenger side and he let out a long, slow breath, trying to ease the tension in his body.

Being with her once hadn't helped at all. One night hadn't been enough.

But there wouldn't be another night. There would be no point to it.

CHAPTER TEN

"THANK you for doing that," Zack said, once they were back in the car and away from the presence of the man they were putting on the show for.

Dinner had gone well, and it looked like everything was on track for Mr. Amudee to sign the exclusive deal with Roasted. It turned out he was thrilled that Zack was marrying a woman he worked with, a woman who understood and shared his passion for the business. It was one of the things, they'd found out over dessert, that had placed Zack slightly ahead of his rival at Sand Dollar. Because Amudee felt Zack and Clara were working together, and the owner of the other coffee-shop chain would be spending more time away from his family.

So, just another way their farce had helped. She still didn't feel good about it.

"You're welcome."

"I'm serious. I should have thanked you before."

"Gourmet dinner after a week in Thailand? I'm not all that put out by it." A big lie, and they both knew it.

"I'm sorry about earlier," she said. "About freaking out about the dress."

"Not a big deal."

Tension hung thick in the air between them. She just felt… restless and needy. The kiss, the one they'd shared in his office, still burning her lips.

It was only supposed to be the one time. Just once. In Chiang Mai, not here.

"I really liked my…salmon," she said. It was lame but she didn't want to leave Zack yet. Didn't want to get into her cold, empty bed and slowly die, crushed beneath the weight of her sexual frustration.

A dramatic interpretation of what would actually happen, but she felt dramatic.

"You didn't have salmon."

"I didn't?" she asked.

"No. You had…I think you had chicken."

"Oh."

The only thing she could remember about dinner was trying not to melt every time Zack looked in her direction.

"So…I guess I'll see you tomorrow, then," she said slowly, reaching for the door handle.

"Wait." She froze. "I have a nice vintage wine at my house. I've been meaning to have you come and try it," he said.

She moved away from the car door, letting her back rest against the seat again. "Really?"

"Yes. Do you want… You could come over and have some?"

Zack could have cut his own tongue out. As pickup lines went, it was a clumsy one. He shouldn't be handing her pickup lines at all, clumsy or otherwise. They'd committed to only sleeping together one time, and the fact that he was so turned on his entire body had broken out into a cold sweat shouldn't change that. Once should have been enough. But it wasn't.

He watched her face, watched her eyes get round, her mouth dropping open. As if she'd just realized what the hidden question was.

It was hidden. If she said no, they could both pretend that it wasn't another night he was after. They could brush it under the rug. Simple.

"Now?" she asked.

He nodded once.

"I don't…" She looked at her apartment building for a moment, her hands folded in her lap, toying with the fabric of her skirt, twisting it. "I'd love some wine."

"Good."

He turned the key over and the engine purred as he pulled away from the curb and headed out of the city, toward the waterfront.

Zack's house was a marvel, grand and pristine, massive windows with views the bay and the Golden Gate Bridge. It was a physical testament to the wealth he'd accumulated since he started his business. How much he had done. How far he had come on his own.

Every time she came over, she stopped and looked at the gorgeous, stained-glass skylight in the entryway. Not this time, though. This time, she didn't have energy to focus on anything beyond Zack and the desire that was roaring through her body. Desire that was finally going to be satisfied tonight.

A week without him, without him inside of her body, had been far too long of a wait.

He closed the door behind them and stood still, poised near the door. He looked like a predator lying in wait. The thought of it, of being the object of his desire, heated her from the inside out.

When he moved, it was quick and fluid. He wrapped his arms around her, kissing her deep and long, his tongue stroking against hers, the evidence of his arousal hard and tempting against her body.

"You're sure?"

"No," she said.

"I'm not, either."

"But I want to."

"Me, too. You know where the bedroom is," he said.

"I do. But I haven't spent that much time in it."

"You'll be lucky if I let you out of it tonight," he said, his voice a low growl. Feral and uncontrolled. It sent a shiver of pure need all the way down to her toes.

It was crazy. Stupid crazy and not at all what they'd agreed to.

Just one more time. One more night.

"I don't mind."

She walked ahead of him, to the winding staircase that led up to his room. She heard him following behind her as she walked up the stairs, and she knew the action was making her dress ride up, made it hug the curve of her bottom, and barely covered it at all.

He grabbed her arm and turned her to him. He was on the step below her, which, with her heels, made them close to the same height. He put his hand on her lower back and pressed her to him, kissing her again, his mouth hot and hungry on hers.

She cupped his face, his stubble rough on her fingertips, a potent, sexy reminder of his masculinity. He reached up and took her hands, lacing his fingers through hers and backing her against the wall as he stepped up onto the stair she was on.

He pressed his body against hers, hard and long, perfectly muscular. She started working the buttons on his shirt, popping a few of them off in her haste to get him undressed. He helped with the sleeve cuffs and tossed the shirt down to the bottom of the stairs.

"Oh, yes," she breathed, running her hands over his bare chest, the crisp hair tickling her palms. "You're so hot."

He chuckled. "I could say the same." He gripped the zipper tab of her dress and tugged it down, letting her dress fall off her body. She hardly had time to think about it, to worry about how she looked to him.

She kicked the dress down to the next stair, still wearing her heels, a strapless bra and a pair of underwear that may as well not exist for all that they covered.

But tonight, she really did feel sexy. She didn't feel the need to cover herself, to hide anything. And she really didn't want him hiding anything. She made quick work of his slacks, pushing them down his muscular thighs, her body heating when she looked at him, dressed in nothing more than a pair of tight black boxer briefs that revealed the outline of his erection in tantalizing detail.

She put her hand on him, sliding her palm over his cloth-covered length, reveling in his harsh, indrawn breath.

"Do you know how many times I thought of you?" she asked, the question requiring a whole lot of boldness she hadn't realized she possessed. "Of touching you. Having my way with you. You've kept me up a lot of nights, Zack. Imagining what it would be like if you kissed me."

"You thought of me?" he asked, his words rough.

"I did."

He didn't have to ask why she hadn't acted on it. Because what would the point have been? They didn't want the same things. He wanted a loveless marriage, no family. She wanted more. There was still no point to this. No point beyond trying to satisfy the sexual hunger that was burning between them.

And the burning hope in her that she couldn't quite snuff out that wondered if he could change his mind...

"Do you know what *I've* thought about?" She pushed his underwear down and he kicked them down with the growing pile of clothes on the staircase. She started to kneel down in front of him and he forked his fingers through her hair, halting her for a moment, the sting from the tug on her hair sending a sharp sensation of pleasure through her.

"Careful," he said. "I'm close."

"We have all night. I'm not worried. And I've had a lot of fantasies about this. You wouldn't deny me a little fantasy fulfillment, would you?" She leaned forward and flicked the tip of her tongue over the head of his shaft. He sucked in a breath, his hold on her hair tightening again.

She took him into her mouth, loving the taste of him, the

power she felt. That she could make his thigh muscles shake, make his hands tremble. He kept one hand in her hair, one on the staircase railing, bracing himself as she continued to explore him.

"Clara...I need...not like this."

She raised her head, her heart nearly stopping when she saw his face. He had sweat beads on his forehead, the tendons in his neck standing out. He looked like a man who'd been tortured with pleasure.

And she'd been the one doing the torturing.

"I don't mind."

"I do. I need to have all of you."

"Maybe we can make it the rest of the way up the stairs?"

"If we hurry," he growled.

So she did, walking in front of him, knowing her thong and high heels were making a provocative visual for him. The feeling of confidence she felt, the absolute certainty that he enjoyed looking at her, that, for now at least, she was the woman he desired, was amazing. New.

His bedroom door was open, and she walked inside and sat down on the bed, waiting for him. He stood in the doorway, his eyes hot on her. The lights were off, moonlight filtering through the window. The darkness felt like a cover, made her feel more confident.

"Take everything off," he bit out.

She undid the front clasp on her bra and was gratified by the sharp rise and fall of his chest as she revealed her breasts to him. She stood and tugged her underwear down her legs, leaving the high heels for last.

"Want to help with these?" she asked, sitting again, holding her foot out.

He smiled and walked over to the bed and knelt in front of her, putting his hands on the curve of her knees, sliding them down her calf, he bent his head down and kissed her ankle as he took one of her shoes off and dropped it onto the carpet.

He did the same with the other one, slow, erotic movements making her shiver all over. And when he leaned in and pressed his mouth between her thighs she nearly came apart with the first stroke of his tongue.

"I'll confess, I didn't think about this very much until recently," he said. "But I haven't stopped thinking about it since last week. Every night, I dream of you," he said, his voice rough as he continued to pleasure her with his hands.

"Me, too," she said, panting, her body on the brink of climax, so close she felt it all through her, tension drawing all of her muscles tight.

Zack stood up, his smile wicked as he looked at her. He leaned over and took a condom from the nightstand. He tore the packet open and rolled a condom onto his length before joining her on the bed.

He put his hands on her thigh and pulled her over him so that her legs were bracketing his and his erection poised at the entranced to her body. Her eyes locked with his, she lowered herself onto him, a low moan climbing in her throat as he filled her.

She gripped his shoulders, enjoying the feeling. Enjoying the moment of being joined with him completely.

She moved slowly at first, trying to find the right rhythm, her confidence increasing as his grip on her hips tightened, as she started to move closer to the edge of climax.

She was saying things, words, about how good it felt, how much she cared about him, but she wasn't sure what she was saying exactly. She didn't care. She couldn't think, she could only feel.

Could only hold on to Zack as her orgasm pushed her over the edge and into an abyss of light and feeling, where there was nothing, no one, except for her and Zack. There was no past, and there was no future. There was only the two of them.

In that world, in that moment, everything could work. Everything was perfect.

The ascent back to reality was slow and fuzzy, and she almost regretted it when it happened. But even reality, his skin hot and sweaty beneath her cheek, his chest hair a little bit scratchy, was pretty near perfect.

She didn't have the assurance of a future. But for now she had Zack. And she would take him. She felt tears sting her eyes and she squeezed them shut, trying to hold them at bay.

She had him tonight. And it would be perfect. She wouldn't ruin it by crying.

"I'll go and take care of things," he said.

Clara sat up and let Zack get out of bed and go into the bathroom. He came back a couple of moments later and slid back into bed. She looked at his profile. Strong, set. So handsome, so special to her. For so long she'd imagined that she knew everything about Zack. Now she found out there was a huge piece missing.

"Zack…" She knew she probably shouldn't say what was on her mind, but they were naked and in bed together. If they couldn't be honest now, when could you be honest with anyone? "What happened?"

"I told you," he said, his voice stilted. He knew what she meant. No need to clarify.

"Sort of."

"You want to hear more?"

"I want to know what happened. Have you ever told anyone?"

There was a long pause, Zack shifted next to her. "I don't talk about this, Clara. Not ever. Not with anyone."

She put her hand on his shoulder. "And I don't let men see me naked. Not ever. But I let you. So tell me."

He paused and she thought, for a moment, he wasn't going to say anything. "We named him Jake. He lived for forty-eight hours. No one at the hospital thought, even for a moment, that he had a chance. But I did." Silence hung between them, heavy and oppressive. She didn't interrupt it.

Zack breathed in deeply. Faintly, in the dim light filtering in through the windows, she could see a single track of moisture shining on his cheek. "I was wrong. There was no miracle. No beating the odds. I'd thought…I was sure he'd have to be okay. I'd changed all my plans, in my head, my whole future was different. And then it was back to being the same, except it wasn't. It never would be again. And my parents…I think they were relieved. They'd been so angry that I was throwing my future away. I think they were relieved when my son died, Clara."

"Zack…" She started to offer something. Comfort maybe. But she wasn't sure if there was any comfort for that kind of pain. She wasn't sure if it was a wound that could heal.

"Sarah didn't want to talk to me again and I don't blame her. Every time I looked at her I just remembered. I think it was the same for her. So I just left. I couldn't stay there." He paused for a moment. "He would be fourteen now. Just two years younger than I was when he was born. Maybe he'd play football, like I did. He'd be close to the age where I would be teaching him how to drive and telling him about girls. I think about it still. About him. I didn't understand how one person could, even for such a short amount of time, became my whole world. For those two days, I breathed for him. And when he stopped, I almost forgot why I was still trying. Rock bottom is…something else. There's a lot of alcohol there, let me tell you. But not even that fixes it. It just makes you pathetic. But I got hired on at a coffeehouse here, even though I was an aimless wreck. Once I had that job, I had a new focus. I got my GED, I found out I loved coffee. I worked my way up in the company, and I bought it from my boss when he retired. I think that's the beginning of what you, and everyone else, already knew."

She wiped at a tear that was sliding down her cheek, her heart aching, her entire body aching, real, physical pain tearing at her. She turned to the side and rested her head on his shoulder, her hand on his face. He wrapped an arm around her and held her to him.

"But that changed me," he said, his voice strong. "It made me grow up. Made me move forward. It taught me to value control. Responsibility and planning. It's why I'm here. Why I'm so successful and not some burned out, ex-college football star has-been."

He believed it. She could tell he did. But the road to success had been hard. It had hurt. And along with conviction, she heard the pain in his voice, too.

"Arrogance, impulsiveness. That leads to disaster. It creates grief. Needless grief," he said.

She wished she could tell him how much she loved him, but she knew that it was the last thing he wanted to hear. So she just held him, and let him hold her. Let him offer her comfort, so that he didn't realize she sas offering him everything.

"So," she said after a while, "do you want me to go?"

"I want you here," he said. "Spend the night with me."

"Sure, Zack," she said, breathing a sigh of relief.

He tightened his hold on her and neither of them spoke.

Tonight they were together. She hoped she didn't fall asleep. She didn't want to miss a moment.

Clara rolled over and stretched in the morning, her eyes opening to a familiar sight. Zack's room. Though, it wasn't familiar at all to wake up in Zack's room. Even less familiar to wake up in Zack's room after making love with him all night.

A slow smile spread across her lips, followed by a pang of sadness when she remembered their conversation. When she remembered his story about his son.

She looked at Zack, his eyes still closed. She wished, more than anything, that she could take his pain from him. His grief was something she couldn't begin to understand, the kind of cut it would leave so deep she wasn't sure if it could heal. She knew it couldn't, not really. It would never disappear. He'd said himself it had changed him. Had changed the course of his entire life.

His eyes opened and he smiled. "Good morning."

"Morning."

"So, I guess we should get ready to go to work," she said.

"You think so?"

"Well, it's almost time."

"True," he said, wrapping his arms around her and rolling her beneath him. "But you might be able to go in late today. I know the boss."

"So do I," she said, wiggling underneath him. "He's kind of intense about people being at work on time. A bit anal, even."

His eyebrows shot up. "Really? Well, I have a feeling that he'll look the other way today."

CHAPTER ELEVEN

"I got an invitation in the mail. For me and my wife." Zack walked into her office and tossed a cream-colored envelope onto her desk.

She grimaced. "Don't people read the news?"

"Well, I called the charity putting the event on and I explained to them what happened. Of course, they would still like me to come and buy two dinners at four hundred dollars a plate, so my new fiancée is more than welcome."

"Well, hopefully the deal will be finalized by then," she said, looking down at the spiteful ring. "And I'll be off the hook."

"Good for both of us, but even if you are, you still might like to come. As my friend."

"Right." Yes. They were friends. First and foremost, before the sex stuff. At least in his mind. She was his friend, and he was hers, her very best friend. But he was so much more to her than that.

"It's for charity. Something I've been planning on for a while, though, thanks to everything that's been happening the timing slipped my mind. And I can't take anyone else until all of this is finished."

She noticed he didn't say that he didn't want to take anyone else. Only that he *couldn't.*

Being a bit oversensitive, aren't we? Maybe. Or maybe not.

"When is it?" she asked.

"Thursday. How are things going today? Have you come up with anything to go with the white tea from Amudee's? I'm thinking of a gourmet tea cake. Wondering if we could start making our own preserves. That has definite mass-market appeal. Are you closer to reaching a deal?"

"It looks that way. I'm optimistic. He's a hard man to read but he seems reasonably satisfied that Roasted is run to the sort of standards he likes to see."

"Good." She fought the urge to reach out and touch him, to forge a connection. That would just come across as needy and she didn't want to seem needy. Even if she did feel a little bit needy.

"What's this?" He took a sheet of paper off her desk and she cringed.

"Uh...a list I was making. For my bakery."

Her bakery. The dream that wasn't really her dream. She loved her job at Roasted, but if things didn't work out with Zack she was going to need her escape more than ever.

"Oh. Right." He set it back down. "Working on it during business hours?"

"Or during lunch. Or maybe during business hours, but you know I put my time in," she said stiffly.

"I'm not going to give you special treatment just because we slept together."

His words hung in the air, too loud in the small office, and far too harsh for her already-tender insides.

"Of course not. That would be ridiculous," she said, picking up a stack of unidentified papers from her desk and walking over to the industrial stapler. She punched it down in three places and hoped that they were at least documents that went together. "Why would you do that?"

The truth was, he had always treated her like she was special, and having him say something like that made her feel demoted.

"You know what I meant."

"I guess I don't."

He rounded her desk and cupped her chin with his thumb and forefinger, tilting her face up so that she had to meet his eyes. He leaned in and pressed a light kiss to her lips. He didn't apologize. He didn't say anything. Even so, all of the fight drained out of her.

"I'm going to be busy tonight," he said.

That was probably for the best. Distance was probably a really, really good idea. Because she desperately didn't want it, and that meant she very likely needed it. Because last night was proof neither of them were thinking clearly where the other was concerned.

They'd done it again. And there could be no more sex. None. It was too dangerous for her, too stupid. Too little. It was physical only for Zack, and she wanted more. She needed more.

"All right. Me, too, actually." She'd find something to be busy with. She would. Except, the only people she ever hung out with, besides Zack, were the people she worked with. And it would be hard hanging out with them now when she was lying to them.

Maybe she'd work on some of the tea pastries she'd been thinking of.

"See you tomorrow, then. At work," she said, feeling very accomplished that she was managing to seem cool and aloof about the whole thing.

"See you then," he said, nodding and walking out of the room.

When he left she blew out a breath. The affair, fling, whatever, was supposed to ease some of the tension between them. But if anything, it seemed more intense than it had before.

She looked back down at her list. The items she was choosing for if she opened her own bakery. For if she had to leave Roasted so she could get away from Zack.

She was starting to hope she wouldn't need it.

* * *

Clara put a pan of twelve cupcakes into the oven and closed the rack with her foot. They were pineapple cupcakes which she was intending to pair light, whipped frosting and candied mango on top. They might very well taste like a Caribbean vacation gone wrong, but she was feeling risky.

She was also feeling restless and sad.

It was Monday and normally Zack would come over for a football game neither of them would pay attention to. He would bring takeout, she would provide all things baked and sinful.

She missed that. And she wondered if the status quo hadn't been so bad after all.

Right. Because you were such a sopping, sad mess you made his wedding cake even though it destroyed you to do it. And you've barely had a date since you met the man.

All true.

She growled into the empty room and turned her focus to whipping her frosting. That, at least, was physically satisfying. She dipped an unused spoon into the mix and tasted it. She hit Play on her kitchen stereo system and turned to the pantry humming while she rummaged for a can of pineapple juice.

She heard a sharp knock over the sound of her acoustic-guitar music and she stopped rummaging. She frowned and walked over to the door, peeking through the security window at the top.

Zack was there, looking back down the hall, like he was thinking about leaving. He had a brown paper bag in his hand, his work clothes long discarded in favor of a gray T-shirt and a pair of dark fitted jeans.

Her heart crumpled. Seeing him was almost painful. A reminder of how close they'd been physically. How far apart they were emotionally.

She braced herself for the full impact of his presence and opened the door.

He turned to her, smiling. "Hi."

"I thought you were busy."

That wasn't what she'd intended to lead with, but it had sort of slipped out. Things just seemed to be "happening" around him without her permission a lot lately.

"It turns out it could wait." He slipped past her and stepped into her apartment, depositing his bags of food on the counter and pulling white boxes from it without even asking for permission.

"Why are you…here?"

"It's Monday."

"And?"

"Football." He shrugged as he opened the first container, revealing her favorite, Sweet and Sour Pork. Like nothing had changed.

It was comforting in a very bizarre way. And a tiny bit upsetting, too. She wasn't sure which emotion she was going to let win. She'd give it until after dinner to decide.

"Right." She turned and made her way around the counter, taking plates and utensils out of the cupboard and drawers. Zack dished up the food and neither of them spoke as they took their first few bites.

"You could turn the game on," she said.

Zack walked across the open room and took her remote off the couch, aiming it at the TV and putting it on the local channel broadcasting the event.

"Who's playing?" she asked.

"No idea." He tossed the remote back where it had been and crossed back into the kitchen, taking a seat at one of the bar stools that lined the counter.

"Important enough to come over for, though," she said, looking down at her plate and stabbing a piece of meat with her fork.

"I missed you," he said, his voice rough.

"What…me? You missed me?"

"Yes. We always get together Monday. And I found myself wandering around my house. Thought about turning the game on. But you're right. I don't really care about football, prob-ably a side effect of coming down from the high of being the world's most entitled high-school jock. I didn't really want to watch sports, but I did want to eat dinner. With you."

"I missed you, too, Zack," she said.

His smile. His presence. His arms around her while she slept. But she wasn't allowed to miss that last part. That had to be done. Over.

As for their friendship…she didn't know what she would do without him. But she didn't know if she would ever get over him if he was always around, either.

But she had to be with him, at least until she left Roasted. She would worry about the rest then.

"Making cupcakes?" he asked.

"They're going to be very tropical." She took a bite of fried rice and stood up, walking back into the kitchen to grab the can of pineapple juice she'd been after when he came to the door. "Not sure about them yet."

She punched the top of the tin and drizzled some juice into her frosting, stirring it in slowly.

Zack leaned over the counter and stuck his finger in the bowl. She smacked the top of his hand. "I will frost your butt, Parsons. Keep your fingers out of my mixing bowl."

He held his finger near his lips and gave her a roguish smile. "Is that what the kids are calling it these days?" He licked his frosting-covered finger and her internal muscles clenched in response.

She snorted. "No. I don't know. You know what I meant."

"Yeah."

Her heart fluttered, but it was a manageable amount. "Behave."

He arched one eyebrow. "Can't make any promises."

She rolled her eyes and sat back down to her dinner.

"Heard anymore about the store in Japan?" she asked.

That got Zack rolling on statistics and sales figures and all sorts of things he found endlessly fascinating. She liked that about him. Liked that his job sometimes gave him a glint in his eye that made him look like an enthusiastic kid.

Then he launched into a story about the street performers that had been out in front of the restaurant tonight when he'd picked the food up, which reminded her of the time they'd been all but accosted by a street mime on their way to lunch one day.

She really had missed this. Sharing. Laughing. She loved that he knew her, that he knew all of her best stories, her most embarrassing moments.

The timer pinged for the cupcakes and she got up to check them.

"Finished?" he asked.

"Yes," she said, pulling them out with an oven mitt and setting them on the counter. "But hot." She nearly laughed at his pained expression. "I have some cool ones, though. I know you don't bake, but if you want to frost them you're welcome to."

"I think I can handle that."

"Bear in mind they are highly experimental."

He smiled. "Sounds exciting, anyway."

"Or a potential disaster of epic proportions, but we won't know until we taste them."

She loaded up a frosting bag and handed it to Zack while she set her own up and got started on leaving little stars all over the surface of one of the cupcakes.

Zack sneaked his hand past her and dipped it into the bowl again. She grabbed the spatula and smacked the back of his hand, leaving a streak of white frosting behind. "I said stop!" she said, laughing as he examined the mess she'd left behind.

"But the frosting is the best part."

"You didn't try the cake yet."

He shrugged and raised his hand to his lips cleaning off the frosting she'd left behind, then he moved his finger near her mouth. "Taste?" he asked.

In that moment, it felt like her vision tunneled, reduced to nothing but Zack. The game, the sounds of the whistle, the crowd, the announcers, faded, blood roaring in her ears.

It was innocent. Or it should have been. She tried to tell herself that for about ten seconds. Because there was no female friend on earth, no matter how close, who would have offered what Zack was at the moment.

So it wasn't innocent. She looked up, her eyes clashing with his.

They were dark, intense. Aroused. The air between them seemed to thicken, the only sound her breath. Too loud. Too obvious.

It wasn't innocent at all.

She'd promised herself it wouldn't happen again. That their last night together had been exactly that: their last night together.

It won't happen again. I just need a taste.

She leaned in and slid her tongue along the line of his finger and her entire body tightened when a rough groan escaped his lips. The salt of his skin gave bite to the super-sweet frosting. If her cupcakes were a bust maybe she could just spread it all over Zack…

No.

She pulled back sharply, shaking her head. "Sorry. Just… sorry, I…"

He wrapped his arm around her waist and kissed her, deep and long, his tongue still coated in icing. When he released her, she felt dazed in the very best way.

She licked her lips. "You taste like a pineapple," she said, her breath erratic, her heart pounding.

"Is that a good thing?" His voice sounded strained, like each word was an effort.

"I might have to…test it out again."

He smiled and her stomach curled in on itself. "I'm more than willing to aid you in the testing."

He dipped his head and she closed the distance between them, sliding her tongue over his bottom lip, reveling in the rough groan that rumbled in his chest.

He dipped his fingers back in the bowl and tugged at the hem of her shirt, drawing it over her head. "I feel at a disadvantage," he said, sliding his fingers over her stomach. "Because you got a chance to taste me this way, and I haven't gotten to do the same."

He bent down and slid his tongue over her stomach. She shivered, gripping his shoulders, knowing they were going too far, not sure if she wanted to stop.

He stood and reached behind her, unhooking her bra with one hand. "You're better at that than I am," she said, her voice shaking.

"Good. That's kind of the idea. I'd hate to think you'd be better off doing this for yourself." He cupped her breast and slid his thumb off her nipple, leaving a faint dusting of icing covering her there. He bent his head and circled the tightened bud with his tongue before drawing it into his mouth.

She forked her fingers through his hair, holding his head to her as he continued to lavish attention on her breast.

"Oh, no...I could not do this by myself," she breathed.

He lifted his head and captured her lips, sweetness clinging to his tongue, his grip tight on her hips as he tugged her body against his. "You're beautiful," he said, abandoning her mouth to skim kisses down her neck, across her collarbone.

"You make me believe it."

He raised his head, his expression serious. "You should never doubt it, not for a moment. You make me lose control."

The words hung between them, an admission that held power. Because she knew Zack, and she knew what he prized. His control. Above everything. She knew why now, too. She even understood it. And he was saying that her beauty, her body, took it from him.

"Me?" she asked.

"You," he repeated, his voice hard. "Everything about you." He moved his palm over her breast and she shuddered. "Now that I'm allowing myself to look…I can't stop myself. I can't stop at just looking, I have to touch you, then I have to taste you. And it's still not enough."

Zack's heart raged out of control. It was more than just arousal. His chest burned, the need going so much deeper than sex. It was pleasure and pain, heaven and hell. But he couldn't turn away from any of it. He didn't want to.

This wasn't what was supposed to happen tonight. He'd missed Clara, Clara his friend. The companionship she provided, the safety. She was the one person he ever let his guard down with. The one person he laughed with. Relaxed with.

It wasn't supposed to turn into this. But his desire for her was like a storm, devastating everything in its path. Devastating his control.

And he'd admitted it to her. Because what else could he do? She'd brought him to his knees.

"It's a nice apartment," he said, trying to lighten the moment, to bring himself back to earth. "I bet the bedrooms are really nice."

She snorted a laugh and buried her face in his neck. "You've been in my bedroom."

He sifted her hair through his fingers. "I've never slept in your bed."

"Do you want to?" She posed the question as though she was asking if he wanted something purely innocent.

"After we get some other business taken care of."

"I'm in complete agreement with that."

He swung her up into his arms and she squeaked, looping her arms around his neck and laughing as he dashed to her bedroom.

Zack set Clara down when they got inside her room. A room he'd been in more times than he could count. But never like this. She kissed him, her mouth hungry, pulled his shirt off him in one swift motion. Trading piece of clothing for piece of clothing until they were both naked, limbs entwined, her full breasts pressed against his chest.

It was almost enough for a while, to simply lay on the bed with her, moving his hands over her bare curves, kissing her. Doing nothing more than kissing.

It was almost enough, but not quite.

He swore sharply. "I don't have anything. I didn't plan this."

"It's okay," she said, wrapping her hand around his length, squeezing him. He groaned, her soft flesh against his almost making up for the fact that he couldn't be inside her. Almost.

He put his hand between her thighs and drew his fingers over her clitoris, then repeated the motion.

She gasped and arched against him, tightening her hold on his arms, fingernails digging into his skin. "Oh, Zack," she breathed, his name on her lips like balm to his soul.

Everything after that was lost in a frenzy of movement, sighs and graphic words that he'd never heard come from Clara's mouth before. But it was only more exciting, because it was her. Because he knew that he was able to do that to her, to make her say things, feel things no other man ever had.

They reached the peak together, his body shaking down to his bones as he found his release.

He held her soft body against his afterward, a sort of strange contentedness spreading through him that he'd never felt before.

"You're beautiful, you know?" he asked, pushing her hair to one side and kissing her neck.

She turned to look at him, rolling to her side, making the curve of her hip rounder, her waist smaller. And her breasts...

"You keep saying that."

"So that you can't doubt it."

"I'm starting to believe you, actually," she said, a smile curving her lips. She reached out and put her finger on his biceps, tracing a long line up to his shoulder. "You're not so bad yourself."

"I'm flattered." He leaned forward and kissed her nose, the contentedness morphing into something else. Something that felt light and…happy.

He wrapped his arms more tightly around her and rolled onto his back. She planted her palms on his chest, her body half on his.

"Hi," she said, smiling.

"I just want you to know that you're not second to anyone," he said, cupping her cheek. "There's no other woman on earth I would rather be with."

Her brown eyes glistened. "You really are good for my ego."

"I'm glad. Someone has to be."

He wanted to say something. Something bigger than he should, than he could. He just wanted more. In that moment, with her body, so soft and bare and perfect, pressed against his, with her smiling at him like he could solve all of the world's problems, he wanted to offer her the world. He wanted more than temporary, more than distant for the first time in his memory.

She rested her head on his chest, her fingertips moving lightly over his skin until her breathing deepened and her eyes fluttered closed.

It wasn't until she was asleep that panic slammed into him. The full enormity of what had happened. He'd lost control. More than that, he'd been letting go of it, inch by inch, with Clara for the past seven years.

With everyone else he was guarded. He never dropped his defenses. He never talked about his past.

He'd cried in front of her. He had allowed real, raw weakness and emotion to escape in her presence when he never even let himself give in like that in private. She was under his skin. So much so she felt like she was a part of him.

A necessary part.

What if he lost her? No, it wasn't even a matter of if, it was when.

The terror that thought evoked, the absolute, gut-wrenching horror was a sobering as a punch to the jaw. He was playing a game he had no business playing, flirting with things he shouldn't be. Tempting feelings he couldn't risk having.

He slid out of her hold and she stirred briefly, stretching, arching her back. His mouth dried. He shook his head and bent to collect his clothes, dressing and walking out of her bedroom, closing the door quietly behind him, ignoring the continual stab of pain in his chest.

He paused in her living room for a moment, the weight of the familiarity of his surroundings crushing him, a feeling of claustrophobia overtaking him.

He had to leave. He had to think. He had to find his control.

He walked out her front door, closing it behind him and making sure everything was locked so that she would be safe. He walked out into the cold night, sucking in a deep breath and blaming the cold for the pain that came with it.

"Where were you this morning? When did you leave?" Clara whispered the words when she went into Zack's office in the early afternoon. He'd been out of the office all morning, and he had been very noticeably not at her apartment before that.

"I had some things to do," he said, his voice flat. "Could you bring me a coffee?" His phone rang and he picked it up. She stomped out of the room and picked up the freshly brewed pot that was sitting in the main area of the office. She poured a half a cup and dumped powdered creamer in, no sugar, and stirred it halfheartedly with one of the little wooden sticks that was on the coffee station.

There were still little lumps of powder floating on the top.

She went back into his office and plunked it onto his desk, letting some of it slosh over the side. He didn't flick her or the coffee a glance as he continued his phone call. He picked it up and took a sip then grimaced and set it back down, shooting her an evil look. She responded with a wide, saccharine smile.

"I'll call you back," he said into the phone, hanging up. "Do you have something on your mind?"

"Yes. Where were you this morning, and do not give me another half-assed answer."

"Clara, there's a way I conduct physical relationships. I don't always stay for the whole night."

She felt like he'd slapped her. Like she was just the same as every other physical relationship he had. But she wasn't. She knew she wasn't.

Anger made her scalp feel prickly. "Don't give me that. Don't even try. I made you shake last night. Made you lose control." Boldness came from anger, and she could't regret it.

His eyes glittered and he looked like he might pounce on her. But he didn't. "I just went home, so that I could get a good night's sleep. I have to go over some legalese in the contract I'm having drawn up for the deal with Amudee. That's all."

That wasn't all. She knew it wasn't all. But she didn't know what the rest of it was, either, so that didn't help.

"And that looks like it's going to go through?" she asked, looking down at the ring again, the ring she was starting to hate, willing to let the subject drop, for now.

"Looks like, but nothing is finalized. So we're still in this until the ink is dry."

She nodded. "I know."

It was all about the contract to Zack. Last night…she could have sworn that last night something had changed. There had been more in their lovemaking. There had been fun. Their friendship had been in it.

It had been special.

Well, today things felt different. It just wasn't the sort of different she'd been hoping for.

"I'll be down in the kitchen," she said, eager to get away.

It was going to take a whole lot of cupcakes to make this day feel okay.

The next few days Zack really did manage to be busy and stay busy. He didn't stop by her apartment late at night, or any time of day. Her head hurt and her bed felt empty. Which was silly, since her bed had been empty of anyone other than her for twenty-five years.

It was just the past couple weeks she'd had Zack sometimes. And she found she really liked it, and it wasn't just because of the orgasms. It was just listening to him breathe. Feeling his body heat so close to hers. Just being with him, finally, finally able to express how much she wanted him. To not have to hold such a huge part of herself back from him anymore.

She loved the way he made her feel about herself. That he wanted her in a sexy red dress, or yoga pants, or nothing. That he made her feel beautiful. That he made her see things in herself she hadn't seen before.

And if she told him that he'd undoubtedly run away screaming.

Tonight, the contracts remained unsigned and that meant they still had plans to go to the big charity event. Something to do with a children's hospital. She wondered if that was by design. If it would bother him. Make him think of his son.

Her heart hurt every time she thought of Zack's past. Of what that false front of his was created to hide. To hide what he'd been through, who he really was. He had perfected a persona, controlled, light, charming, and even she had bought into it. Not even *she* had seen everything.

But she was starting to.

Tonight was going to feel more like a real date. A public event with just the two of them, not with Mr. Amudee sitting by, watching their performance as a couple. She was dressing up in a dress she'd selected this time. Something between her usual fare and that screaming, sex-on-a-hanger number Zack had picked out for her.

It was a full-length gown with a mermaid-style skirt that conformed to her body before flaring out around her knees. It swished when she walked, and a halter-top neckline showed her cleavage. And she felt sexy in it. She felt like a woman who was ready to conquer the world. One who could outshine other women, at least for the man she was with. And that was what mattered, anyway.

She heard a knock on her door and she tried to shove her feet into stilettos, while standing, and fastening dangly diamond earrings. "Coming!"

She opened the door and all the air rushed out of her body. Zack was a wearing a suit, black jacket, crisp white shirt and a perfectly straight black tie. He was the epitome of gorgeous. He always was, half dressed, all dressed or completely naked. But there was something about a man in a suit…

It sort of reminded her of his wedding. The wedding that wasn't.

"You look…you look great," she said.

"So do you. I brought you something," he said.

There was something strange about his tone, something formal and distant. It matched his clothing. Cool, well-tailored, nothing out of place. And yet, that in and of itself felt out of place. Zack wasn't formal with her. Why should he be? They'd known each other for years. They had slept together for heaven's sake.

She held her hand out and smiled, trying to make him smile. It didn't work.

He took a flat, black box from his jacket and opened it.

"Oh, my…Zack this is…it must have cost…" None of her words would gel into a complete sentence, everything jumbling and stalling half thought through.

It was a necklace, a truly spectacular necklace, not the sort you saw under the display case of just any department store.

Not even the sort of thing you saw at Saks. It was too unique, too extravagant.

She reached out and touched the center stone, a deep green emerald, cut into the shape of a teardrop and surrounded by glittering diamonds.

"I don't think I can accept this."

"Of course you can," he said, his voice still tinged with that unfamiliar distance. "Turn around."

She did, slowly, craning her neck to look at him. He swept her hair to the side and took the necklace from the box, draping it over her, the stone falling between her breasts, the chill making her shiver. He clasped the necklace, his fingers brushing the back of her neck as we worked the tiny clasp.

"This isn't...this isn't a friendships gift," she said, her voice trembling.

That did earn her a short chuckle. "Maybe tonight friendship isn't what I want."

His words made her shiver, the sensual promise in them turning her on. The underlying, darker meaning she couldn't quite grasp making goose bumps break out on her arms. "It really is too much," she said, turning to face him, her nose nearly touching his.

He straightened putting some distance between them. "It's a perfectly fitting gift for a lover. Are you ready?"

"Yes," she said, turning his choice of word over in her head. Yes, she was his lover, in the sense that they'd slept together. But there was something in the way he said it, something that seemed cold, when a lover should be something warm. Something personal.

She touched the necklace, the gems cold beneath her fingertips.

CHAPTER TWELVE

THE charity ball was crowded already when they arrived, a sea of beautiful people dressed in black positioned around the ballroom, chatting and eating the very expensive canapes.

Heads turned when she and Zack walked down the marble staircase and down into the room. Everyone was looking at Zack, because it was impossible not to. She was fully appreciating just how he was viewed in the community now. A man of power and wealth, a man of unsurpassed beauty. If you could call what he possessed beauty. It was too masculine for that, and yet she wasn't sure there was another word for it, either.

Pride flared in her stomach, low and warm. All the women in the room were looking at Zack with undisguised sexual hunger. And Zack was with her. Touching her, his hand low on her back, possessive.

She turned and pressed a kiss to his cheek. He looked at her. "What was that for?"

"Because," she said.

He looked at her for a moment, a strange light in his eyes. "Let's go find our table."

"Okay," she said, trying to ignore the tightening in her throat.

There was a table, for two, with place cards set on each empty plate. Zack held her chair out for her and she sat, her heart slamming against her ribs as she read the name that had been written in calligraphy on her place card.

Hannah Parsons.

With Zack's name tacked on to hers, even. Clara felt dizzy. She looked down at the ring. Hannah's ring. Hannah's seat. Hannah's man. She had to wonder if the necklace had been meant for Hannah, too.

She wrapped her fingers around the card and curled them into a fist, crumpling it and tossing it onto the marble floor.

"What the hell?" Zack asked.

"It had the wrong name on it," she said stiffly.

"Does it matter?"

That hit even harder than seeing the name. "I suppose not." She put her foot over the crumpled paper and squished it beneath the platform of her stiletto.

"You're the one who's here with me." He stretched his hand toward hers, covering it, stroking her wrist. "No one else."

She knew it. And in some ways she knew his words were sincere. But there was also something generic in them. There was something strangely generic to the whole evening and she couldn't quite place what it was or why.

"Of course." She looked into his eyes, tried to find something familiar now. Something of her friend. But she didn't see it. She only saw the man as he presented himself to the world. Aloof, put together, charming. But there was no depth there. No feeling or warmth.

It was frightening.

Dinner was lovely, tiny bits of sculpted beauty made to be admired before being eaten. Of course it was marked up extravagantly, because the whole point of the evening was that the charity received donations.

A woman in a long, flowing dress walked up onto the stage, her air of authority making it obvious that she was the coordinator of the event, and a hushed silence fell over the crowd.

"Thank you all for coming tonight," she said. "And for the

very generous donation of your time and money to the Bay Area Children's Hospital."

She turned and looked toward their table, a smile on her face. "And tonight, we would also like to give special acknowledgment to Mr. Zack Parsons, who has donated enough money to revamp the entire Neo-Natal Intensive Care Unit. Everything in the unit will be state of the art. It will be the best equipped facility in the state of California. There have been major advances in the field of Neo-Natal medicine over the past few years. We're able to offer hope to babies, to families, who wouldn't have had any as little as five years ago. And now, we're able to offer even more. So, thank you, Mr. Parsons."

The room erupted into applause and everyone stood. Except for Zack. Except for her. Her eyes stung, her entire body feeling numb.

Zack lifted his hand and nodded once, his acknowledgment. Her heart broke for him. What a wonderful gift he was giving to so many families. A gift he hadn't been able to give to himself, to his own son.

She wanted to howl at the universe for the unfairness of it all. And yet there was no point. And Zack was there, broken, and probably in pain. She could be there for him. It was all she could do. And she would. Because she was his friend. His lover.

The speaker went on to talk about some more donations and then invited everyone to stay for dancing and an open bar.

After the applause died away, people started to wander around the room, talking and laughing, some people came to talk to Zack. She wanted to tell them to go away. Because she could feel the dark energy, the grief, radiating from him like a physical force. How was everyone else missing it?

She didn't understand how they could miss what was so clear to her.

"Let's go." She put her hand on his, felt his pulse, pounding hard in his wrist. She ran her fingers along his forearm.

She didn't think he would accept loving words, but she could offer him comfort in another way. A way he could accept.

There was no question where things would end up tonight. No fighting it. They both knew it.

He nodded once and stood, she stood, too, and went to him, putting her hand on his back. He wrapped his arm around her waist as they headed out of the ballroom.

Zack's chest felt too full. Everything felt like too much. The whole day. He shouldn't have brought Clara with him tonight. It was one thing to sit in a room full of strangers and have them talk about his contribution to the NICU, but it was another to have someone sitting there, knowing why he'd done it. Someone else thinking of Jake. It was hard enough to be alone in it. Sharing it made it seem more real. It made him feel exposed.

It made him feel like everything, his failures, his pain, was written on him. Something he couldn't hide, or scrub off no matter how many layers of control he tried to conceal it with.

Clara saw him.

When he'd picked her up tonight, he'd fully intended on keeping her at a distance, putting her in her place. A new place. Because he had mistresses, women who were with him for the sole purpose of warming his bed and accompanying him to events.

He wasn't friends with those women. He didn't eat their baked goods, he didn't know that they wore yoga pants to bed when there wasn't a man around. He didn't know that they were insecure about their bodies, or that their favorite band was still that group of long-haired teenage boys that had been so popular in the nineties.

He didn't know anything about them beyond what they looked like naked.

He knew the other stuff about Clara. And he knew the naked stuff. And tonight he'd been determined to focus only on the

latter. If he couldn't keep her as only a friend, and he'd proven
he wasn't doing a very good job of that, then he would have her
as a mistress. Because what had happened at her apartment, the
way they'd shared dinner, jokes, then made love, him holding
her while she'd slept…he couldn't do that. It was too reckless.
To out of his control.

He had to move her into the compartment he could deal
with. And she seemed determined to push her way back out.

The expression on her face when she saw the wrong card
in her spot had been so sad, stricken, as though someone had
slapped her.

And he'd felt it in him. As though her emotion was his. He'd
always felt connected to Clara, but this was different. Sharper.
Impossible to deny. Beyond his control.

He should have taken her home. Yet he'd still taken her back
to his house. Because he had planned on having her tonight,
had been obsessed with it all week. If only to prove that he
could sleep with her without having his insides flayed. Sex was
only sex. It didn't have to be personal, it didn't have to mean
anything. It didn't have to be related to the awful, tight feeling in his chest.

She was beautiful tonight, incredible in that form-fitting
black dress and the gem, enticing in the valley of her cleavage, drawing his eye, tormenting him.

She was standing by the massive living-room windows, the
bay in the background, city lights glittering on the inky surface
of the waves. He wanted her. Here and now. A good thing he'd
planned for it. It wasn't spur-of-the-moment, it wasn't beyond
his control.

He had condoms and everything else he needed. He was in
control. He desperately needed the control. He tightened his
hand into a fist, steadied it, ignored the tremor that ran through
his fingers and skated up his arm, jolting his heart.

Ignoring the strange tenderness he felt when he looked at

her. This wasn't about feeling, not in an emotional sense. This was physical. It was sex.

"Take off your dress," he said.

She reached behind herself and unzipped the gown, letting it fall to the floor. She wasn't wearing a bra, only a small triangle of lace keeping her from being completely bare. That and the necklace, the emerald heavy and glittering between her breasts.

She reached around to remove it, her breasts rising with the action, pink tipped and perfect.

"No," he ground out. "Leave it on." A reminder. A reminder that she was the same as every other woman he'd ever been with. The exchange of gifts, jewelry, that was how it worked. It was invariable, it was safe. It was unchallenging.

She dropped her hands to her sides and he walked closer to her, loving the way the moonlight spilled silver over her pale curves. The way the deep shadows accentuated the dip of her small waist, the round fullness of her hips and breasts.

She was a woman. There was no denying it. And he was starving for her.

But he would wait. He would draw it out. Because he was the master of this game. He was always in charge. He had forgotten that sometimes over the past few weeks, had allowed her inexperience, the nature of their friendship, to change the way he approached it.

Not now.

She's a woman. Only a woman. The same as any other.

No. Not the same. His mind rebelled against that thought immediately. There had never been a more exquisite woman, that much he knew for certain. There had never been a figure, not since Eve, better designed to tempt a man.

She was the epitome of sensual beauty, more seductive simply standing there than any other woman could have been if she'd been trying.

Clara.

Her name flashed through his mind, loud, a reminder.

No. He didn't need it. He wasn't thinking of her. Only of his own need and how she might fulfill it. He would pleasure her, too, as he did all of his lovers. But it wasn't different. It couldn't be different. Not again. Not after that night in her apartment.

"Turn around for me," he said. "Face the window."

She obeyed again. She was like a perfect hourglass, the elegant line of her back enticing. He walked over to her, extending his hand and tracing the dip of her spine. She shivered beneath his touch.

"Do you like that?" he asked.

"I've liked everything you've ever done to me." Her voice, so sweet, a bit vulnerable. Not a temptress.

Clara.

He put his hands on her hips and tugged her back against him, let her feel the hard ridge of his arousal, the blatant, purely sexual evidence of what he wanted from her. Her indrawn breath, the short, sweet sound of pleasure that escaped her lips, let him know that she was tracking with him. Important.

He would never do anything she didn't want.

He put his hand on her stomach, soft, slightly rounded. He liked that about her, too, that she was so feminine, curved everywhere. Absolute perfection.

He cupped her butt with his other hand, her flesh silken beneath his palm. "You're beautiful," he said. She leaned back against him, her head against his chest. Her slid his hand up to palm her breast, teasing her nipples as he continued to stroke her backside.

He gripped the side of her panties and drew them down her legs.

He move his hand back behind her, moving it forward, teasing her slick folds before parting them and sliding his fingers deep inside of her. She gasped, spreading her thighs a bit wider to accommodate him.

The line of her neck was so elegant, irresistible. He bent his head and kissed her there, tasting the salt of her skin, so familiar now, as he slid his free hand up to her breast and squeezed her nipple tightly between his thumb and forefinger. She arched against him, her breathing growing harsher, more shallow.

He had her pleasure in his hands, how he touched her and where, dictating everything she did. Everything she felt. This was like everything else. Every other sexual encounter he'd had as an adult. He was in charge of their pleasure, both of them. He decided when things happened and how.

This thing with Clara hadn't been right from the beginning, because he hadn't managed to put her in her place for their affair. He hadn't separated their friendship from it. That was why he'd shared with her, held her while she slept. That was why he'd started feeling things.

But he knew it now. He knew what he had to do. He could still have her. He could get a handle on everything, and then he could have her. He touched the necklace between her breasts, fingers sliding over the gem. A reminder of exactly what they had between them.

She tried to turn and he held her so she was facing the window, away from him. He reached over and picked up a condom sheathing himself and turning her to the side so that she was standing in front of the couch.

"Hold on to the back of it," he said. She obeyed, bending at the waist, gripping the back of the couch. She looked back at him, her eyes round, questioning. Familiar.

He chose not to focus on her face. He gripped her hips, looked at the curve of her hips, how her body dipped in beautifully, perfectly, at her waist.

He positioned himself at the entrance to her body.

She made a short, low sound that vibrated through her. "Okay?" he asked, his teeth gritted tight, every ounce of control spent on moving slowly, on not thrusting in to her the rest of the way and satisfying the need that was roaring inside of him.

"Yes," she said.

He pushed into her the rest of the way, her body so hot and tight it took every ounce of his willpower to keep from coming the moment he was inside.

"Oh, Zack," she breathed. "Zack."

His name on her lips, her voice, so utterly Clara. So familiar and still so exciting.

Clara. Her name was in his head on his lips, with each and every thrust, with each sweet pulse of her internal muscles around his shaft.

And suddenly there was no denying it. It didn't matter that he couldn't see her face. Her smell, the feel of her skin beneath his fingertips, the way it felt to be in her body, all of it was pure, undeniable Clara Davis.

The woman who baked orange cupcakes and had a pink wreath on the door. The woman knew about his past, about the darkest moments of his life. The woman who smiled at him every morning. Who could always make him smile, no matter what. Who put powdered creamer in his coffee when he made her angry.

The woman who lit him on fire, body and soul.

He couldn't pretend she was someone else, or that it didn't matter who she was. There was no way. No one had ever been like her before, no one ever would be.

He had no control. He had nothing. He was at her mercy. If he'd had to get on his knees and beg her for a kiss tonight he would have done it, because he needed her.

Not just in a purely sexual sense. He needed *her.*

His climax built, hard and fast, the pitch too steep, too unexpected for him to control. He put his hand between her thighs and stroked her, trying to bring her with him. Her body tightened around him, her orgasm hitting hard and fast. When she cried out her pleasure, then he let go.

"Clara," he whispered, resting his forehead on her back as he gave in. As he let the release crash through him, devastating everything in its path.

He released his hold on her hips, his body shaking, spent as though he'd just battled his way through a storm. Sweat made his skin slick all over. His hands were trembling, his breathing sharp and jagged.

He looked at her. At Clara. There were red marks on her hips where his fingers had pressed into her flesh. Where he had lost all control. He brushed his fingers along the part where he'd marked her, his chest tightening, regret forming, a knot he couldn't breathe around.

She turned to look at him, a smile on her lips. She straightened, naked and completely unconcerned about it. Nothing like she'd been at first. Her confidence, the fact that she felt beautiful, shone from her face.

Her beautiful face. Unique. Essential. So damn important.

"I'm sorry," he said.

She blushed, looking away from him. "Didn't I tell you not to apologize to me all the time?"

"What about when I need to?" he asked, moving toward where she was standing, brushing his fingertips over her hips. "I was holding on to you too tightly," he whispered.

She met his eyes and they held. He saw deep, intense emotion there. A connection, affection. Something real. It wasn't part of a facade, or a game. It was the way she always looked at him, whether they were in his office, in her living room or in bed. She was the same woman. She cared for him. She looked at him like he mattered to her.

The realization rocked him, filled him. Every piece and fiber of his being absorbing it. It made it easier to breathe, as though he hadn't truly been drawing in breath for years and now he was again.

For the first time in fourteen years. Since he'd lost his reason for breath, his desire to give any sort of emotion, to give of himself. He felt like he'd found it again. In Clara's eyes.

"I didn't mind," she said.

The moment, the tiny sliver of freedom he felt evaporated, chased away by a biting, clawing panic that was working from his stomach up through his chest. He had felt this way before and it had ended in utter destruction.

He knew what this was. And he knew he couldn't have it. Wouldn't allow himself to have it. Not ever. Not ever again.

He took a step away from her and bent down, picking her dress up from the floor, rubbing his fingers over the sequins. He felt choked, like his throat was closing in on itself, like his chest was too full for his lungs to expand.

He could do it. He could have her still, keep her where she belonged in his life. In his bed.

He had been careless again. He had lost control. He could find it again. He had to.

"Get dressed," he said, handing her the gown.

"What?"

"I'll drive you home."

"What?" she said again.

He didn't look at her face. He couldn't.

"You and I are having an affair, Clara, I made that clear the other day. I don't cuddle up with the women I'm having sex with at night, and I damn sure don't have their toothbrush on my sink. That's just how it works."

"And I think I told you, I am not just one of your mistresses."

"When you're in my bed…or my couch, you are."

"I am your friend," she said, her voice ringing in the room.

"Not when we're here, like this. Now, you're just the woman I'm sleeping with. We aren't going to curl up and watch a chick flick after what just happened."

She jerked back, pulling her dress over her breasts. "I'm going to go get dressed. Send the car. I'm not riding back with you, and I'm not staying, not now so I think the decent thing to do, if you still remember decency, would be to arrange me a ride."

"Clara…"

"We'll talk tomorrow. I can't now."

She turned and walked away, her steps clumsy. She ducked into his downstairs bathroom and closed the door. He heard the click of the lock.

And he didn't blame her. But he had to define the relationship, as much for her benefit as for his. Yes, he had lied. She was different. But she couldn't be. It couldn't happen.

He would fix it. He'd gotten it wrong tonight, by denying the one thing that had been there from the beginning. His feelings. The sex…he would pretend it hadn't happened. Whatever he had to do to fix it, to have her never look at him like that again. As if he was a cold stranger, as if he'd physically hurt her.

It would have to go back to how it was. Because he could live without sex. He wasn't sure he could live without Clara.

It was the longest car ride in the world. No one was on the streets, and it technically took half the time it normally did to get from Zack's place to hers, but it seemed like the longest ever.

Because everything hurt. And she was wearing a really fabulous gown that had already been torn from her body once, during the most intense, emotion-filled sexual encounter they'd ever had. There had been something dark in Zack tonight. A battle. She wasn't stupid. She knew something had changed, she knew, at least she hoped, that he wasn't as horrible as he'd seemed when he'd sent her away.

She bunched up the flaring skirt of her gown when the car stopped and she slid out, letting the dress fan out around her. She gave the driver a halfhearted, awkward wave. He knew her. She'd used his services quite a few times with Zack. Having him be a part of this, the most awful, embarrassing, heart-wrenching moment of her life wasn't so great.

Because it was two in the morning and it was completely obvious what had just happened. That Zack had had sex with her, sex, at its most base, and had her go home rather than have her spend the night in his bed.

She curled her hands into fists and let her nails cut into her palms, tears stinging her eyes. She almost hated him right now. It almost rivaled how much she loved him.

Almost.

If she didn't love him, it wouldn't hurt so bad.

You're my mistress.

Like hell she was. He might be the only man who'd seen her naked, but she was certain, beyond a shadow of a doubt, that she was the only woman who'd ever seen him cry.

CHAPTER THIRTEEN

SHE really hoped everyone wanted cupcakes for lunch. Because there were cupcakes. Nine varieties of them, and someone had to eat them.

She didn't think she could eat and she was *not* sharing them with Zack, which meant they would be going straight into the break room. On the bright side, she'd found a few new varieties that had worked out nicely.

The sea-salt caramel one was her favorite. She just couldn't force down more than two bites at a time. Anything beyond that stuck in her throat and joined the ever-present lump that made her feel like she was perpetually on the edge of tears.

She was just too full of angst to eat anything. She hadn't been able to eat anything since she'd been dropped at the front of her building by Zack's driver.

Zack.

She put her head on the pristine counter of the office kitchen and tried to hold back the sob that was building in her chest.

Something had broken in him last night. It had started after their time together at her place, the night he'd left. And last night it had snapped completely. But she didn't know what it was. She didn't know how to pull him out of it. If she could, or if she even should.

"Clara."

Clara looked up and saw Jess standing in the doorway of the kitchen. "Zack is looking for you."

"Oh," Clara straightened and wiped her eyes. Normally Zack would come and find her himself. Because there was a time when he'd wanted to be with her simply to be with her. Now she wondered if she had any value when she wasn't naked. "I'll be there in a second. Take…" She gestured to the platters of cupcakes. "Take some of these with you. I can't eat them by myself. If Zack comes near them, tell him they have walnuts."

Jess's eye widened. "They all have walnuts?"

"No. But tell him they do. All of them."

Jess gave her a strange look and picked two of the platters up, heading back out the door.

She had no choice now. She had to go face the man himself. And figure out exactly what she was going to say. As long as it didn't involve melting into a heap, she supposed almost anything would do.

"You sent Jess after me?" She looked inside of Zack's office, waiting to be invited in. Silly maybe, since she hadn't knocked on his office door in the seven years since she'd started working at Roasted. But she felt like she needed to now.

"Yes. Come in." His tone was formal, like it had been the night before when he'd given her the necklace. Distance. Divorced from emotion.

That was the strange thing. He'd been aloof the night of the charity, until they'd made love. Then he'd been commanding, all dark intensity and so much emotion it had filled the room. It had filled her. It hadn't been good emotion. It had been raw and painful. Almost more than she could bear.

It had caused the break. That much she knew.

But he was back to his calm and controlled self now, not a trace of last night's fracture in composure anywhere. She almost couldn't believe he was the same man whose hands had trembled after they'd made love.

She almost couldn't believe he was the same man she'd known for seven years. The same man she'd watched movies with, shared dinners with.

But he was. He was both of those men.

He was also the cold man standing before her, and she wasn't sure how all of those facets of himself wove together. And she really wasn't sure where she fit in. If she did at all.

She stepped into the office, watching his face for some sort of reaction. He had that sort of distant, implacable calm he'd had on his wedding day, standing and looking out the window as though nothing mattered to him. As though he had no deeper emotion at all.

She knew differently now. She saw it for what it was now. A facade. But she wasn't certain there was a way through it, unless he wanted her to break through.

"I'm about to sign the final paperwork for the deal with Amudee. I wanted to thank you for your help."

For her help. "Of course."

They were talking like strangers now. They'd never been like strangers, not from the moment she'd met him. They'd had a connection from the first moment he'd walked into the bakery.

Now she couldn't feel anything from him. Now that they'd been so intimate, she felt totally shut off from him.

"Once everything is finalized we can let everyone know that our engagement has been called off," he said.

"Right," she said, clenching her left hand into a fist.

"That's all." He looked back at his computer screen for a moment, then looked back up. "Are you busy tonight?"

Her heart stopped. Did he want sex? Again? After what he'd done last night?

"Um...why?"

"Because I thought I might come over and watch a movie."

His words were so unexpected it took her brain a moment

to digest them, as though she was translating them from a foreign language. "And?"

He shrugged. "Nothing."

He was behaving as if…as if nothing had changed. As if
they'd gone back in time a few weeks.

He was pretending, she was certain of it, because he certainly wasn't acting normal, whatever he might think, but she
was insulted that he was trying. After what he'd said to her
last night. After the way he'd objectified her.

She wanted to yell at him. Maybe even hit him, and she'd
never hit anyone in her life. But she wanted a reaction. She
didn't want his control.

"Are you going to pretend last night didn't happen?" she
asked, her voice low, unsteady.

Zack remained calm, his control, that control he claimed
to have lost, the control she witnessed in tatters last night,
firmly in place. "I think we both know that's not working out.
But you're right. You're my friend, and I didn't treat you like
a friend last night."

"An understatement," she spat. "You treated me like your
whore."

She saw something, an emotion, faint and brief, flicker in
his eyes before being replaced by that maddening calm again.
That same sort of dead expression he'd worn when he'd been
jilted on his wedding day.

"I apologize," he said. "I wasn't myself."

She curled her hands into fists, her fingernails digging into
the tender skin on her palm, the pain the only thing keeping
her from exploding. "Do you know what I think, Zack? I think
you were yourself. This? This is the lie. This isn't you. It's you
being a coward. You can't face whatever it is that happened
between us last night and now you're hiding from it."

"It isn't working. That element of our relationship." The only
thing that betrayed his tension was the shifting of a muscle in

his jaw. "But we've been friends for seven years. That works for us. We need to go back to that."

"Are you…are you crazy?" she asked, the words exploding from her. "We can't go back. I've been naked with you. You've been… We've made love. You can't just go back from that like it never happened. I don't care what we thought, we were wrong. That one night, that one night that's turned into four, it changed everything. You can't just experience something like that with someone and feel nothing."

"I can."

"Do you really think this is nothing? That we're nothing?"

"We're friends, Clara. You mean a lot to me. But it doesn't mean I want to keep sleeping with you. It doesn't mean I want this kind of drama. We need things back like they were so that the business can stay on track…."

"I'm leaving Roasted. You know that."

He tightened his jaw. "I didn't think you would really leave."

"What? Now that we've slept together? You can't have it both ways. Either it changed things or it didn't."

"I care about you," he said, his tone intensifying.

"Not enough." She shook her head, fighting tears. They weren't sad tears. She was too angry for that. That would come later. "I am your sidekick, and that's how you like it. As long as I give you company when you want it, eat dinner with you when you're lonely, bake your wedding cake when you decide it's time to have a cold, emotionless marriage, well then, you care about me. As long as I'm willing to pretend to be your fiancée so you can get your precious business deal. But it's on your terms. And the minute it isn't, when I start having power, that's when you can't handle it."

He only looked at her, his expression neutral.

"I'm done with it, Zack," she said, pulling the ring, the ring that wasn't hers, from her finger. "All of it."

She put the ring on his desk and backed away, her heart thundering, each beat causing it to splinter.

"We have a deal," he bit out.

"You'll figure it out. If that's the only reason you don't want me to go…if that's all that's supposed to keep me here… I can't."

Zack stood, his gray eyes suddenly fierce. "So, you're just going to walk out, throw away our friendship over a meaningless fling?"

"No. It's not the fling, Zack, it's the fact that you think it's meaningless. The fact that I've realized exactly where I rate as far as you're concerned."

"What do you want?" he exploded. "Why is what we have suddenly not good enough for you?"

"Because I realized how little I was accepting. That everything was about you. I'm just willing to take whatever you give me, whether it's a spot in your bed or a job baking your wedding cake and it's…sick. I can't keep doing this to myself." She turned to go and he rounded the desk, gripping her arm tightly.

"I'll ask you again," he said, his voice rough. "What do you want? I'll give it to you. Don't leave."

"So I can wait around for you to decide you want to try a loveless marriage again? So I can bake you another cake? Maybe I'll help the bride pick out her dress this time, because, hey, I'm always here to do whatever you need done, right?"

"Does it bother you? The thought of another woman marrying me? Then you marry me." He reached behind him and took the ring off the desk, holding it out to her, his hand shaking. "Marry me. And stay."

She recoiled, her stomach tight, like she'd just been punched. "For what purpose, Zack? So I can be the wife you don't love? Your stand-in for Hannah, different woman, same ring. Doesn't matter, right? You're still doing it. You're trying to keep me from leaving, trying to keep control. You'll even marry me to keep it. That's not what I want."

He took her hand in his, opened it, tried to hand her the ring.

She pulled back. "Don't," she said, her voice breaking. "Don't. I'm going to clean my desk out now."

"Clara."

Zack watched as she turned away from him and walked out his office door, closing it sharply behind her. Everything was deathly silent without her there, his breath too loud in the enclosed space. The ring too heavy.

Had he truly done that? Offered her Hannah's ring? Begged her to marry him just so she would stay?

He had. She had gone anyway and there had been nothing he could do to make her stay. All of his control, all of his planning, hadn't fixed it. He had lost the one person in his life who had given things meaning.

He'd been pretending, from the moment he'd met Clara, that she was only his friend. Only one thing. Because he'd known she could very easily become everything. How had he not realized that she'd been everything from day one?

Pain crashed through him, a sense of loss so great it stole the breath from his lungs.

His chest pitched sharply, his body unable to take in air.

He dropped the ring and it fell to the floor, rolling underneath his desk. He left it. It didn't matter.

He'd just broken the only thing in his life that did matter.

Control. She spoke of his control, how he tried to control her, keep her in his life on his terms. And she was right. Because he'd known instinctively that if he ever let go of that control she would take over.

She had. His control was shattered now, laying around his feet in a million broken pieces he would never be able to reclaim.

And if finding it again meant losing Clara, he didn't want it, anyway.

He hadn't chosen to lose his son, it had been a tragedy, one that had painted his life from that moment forward. He'd let

Clara leave, because he'd been too afraid to give. Too afraid to let his barriers down.

Because he'd been certain he couldn't live with the kind of pain love would bring, not again. But now he was certain he couldn't live without it. Without Clara. He loved her so much his entire being ached with it.

And if he had to lay down every bit of pride, every last vestige of control and protection to have her back, he would.

CHAPTER FOURTEEN

CLARA had looked at nine buildings in the space of four hours. She'd hated them all. The idea of having her own bakery... it had been so great before. But she realized now that when she pictured it, when she saw the image of a shop filled with people enjoying her cupcakes, Zack was there. At a table that she knew, in her imagination, anyway, was the one he sat at every day.

And she would come and sit with him when she took a break. And ask him what his favorite confection was. How his day had been. If he'd run in to any mimes. Because in her mind, in her heart, she'd never truly thought he would be gone from her life altogether.

The truth was, a life without him had been impossible to imagine.

In the three days since she'd walked out of Zack's office, it had changed. She didn't have a vision when she viewed the potential bakery locations. She saw nothing more than brick and wood. There were no visions. No warmth.

There was no Zack.

When he'd handed her the ring...the temptation to say yes had been there, and it had sickened her. That she would continue to be the void filler in Zack's life, while she let him be her everything. It was wrong. And she knew it.

Still, a part of her wished she could go back and say yes. She despised that part of herself.

She sighed and walked up the narrow staircase that led to her apartment. She hadn't taken the elevator in three days, either. Because it reminded her of the elevator rides with Zack, the ones rife with sexual tension. It was almost funny now.

Almost. She'd discovered a broken heart made it mostly impossible to find things funny.

When she reached her floor she walked slowly down the hall. She was exhausted, but going back to her apartment wasn't a restful thought. Because he was everywhere there. Memories of him. On her couch, in the kitchen, most recently, in her bed.

She stopped midway down the hall, her eyes locking on the small pink and brown box placed in front of her door. She eyed it for a moment before making her way to it, kneeling down and lifting the lid.

Her breath caught in her throat when she saw the contents. Cupcakes.

The ugliest cupcakes she'd ever seen. The frosting was a garish orange, the cake a sort of sickly pale gray. There was a note tucked into the side and she took it out and unfolded it.

I know I said I don't bake. I did, though. For you. Because it means something to you and I wanted to try it. It made me feel close to you to do it. Please don't eat them, they're terrible. I miss you.
Zack

She traced the letters with her fingertips, his handwriting so familiar. So dear to her. The note was scattered, funny. Sweet. She could hear him reading it to her.

A tear slipped down her cheek. "I miss you, too," she said. "But I couldn't let things stay the same."

"Don't cry. I know they're awful, but they aren't that bad are they?"

Clara looked up and saw Zack standing in the doorway of the elevator. He looked tired, the lines around his mouth deeper.

She wiped her cheeks. "They're pretty bad."

"Almost as bad as their creator." He took a step toward her. "I'm sorry. About the other day. About the past few weeks."

"Zack can we not do this? I don't think...I don't think I can."

"Well, I can't walk away. I won't. So if you don't mind me camping out here in front of your door until you're ready, then I can wait."

Clara crossed her arms beneath her breasts, curling her hands into fists, trying to disguise that she was shaking, trembling from head to toe. "What is it?"

"I told Amudee that I lied."

"And?"

"We still have a deal, but not based on how he feels about me as a human being. More about my corporate track record."

"Why did you do that?"

"Because I had to clean this up. I used you. I didn't want to gain anything from that."

Clara tried to smile. "I appreciate that, Zack, but..."

"I'm not finished."

She blinked and tried not to cry. She wasn't ready for this. Wasn't ready for him to try to repair their friendship, not when she needed more.

"You were right. About me," he continued. "I have been trying to control everything in my life, including you. Because I felt like there was safety in control. I felt like it was responsible, and I never wanted to deal with the consequences of a lack of control again."

He took a step toward her, put his hand on her cheek, and her heart stopped. "Clara, from the moment I met you I felt a connection with you. And I had to make a very quick decision about where to put you in my life. It was conscious. It was controlled. So I decided you would be my friend, my employee, but never anything more. Because I think part of me knew that if I let you, you could mean everything to me. If I didn't keep you in your place you would fill my life, every part of me. That I would love you. But then in Chiang Mai, being near you like that, I couldn't deny it anymore. I couldn't pretend I didn't want you. And we gave in. I lost control. So then, I thought maybe if I put you in that same place in my head I put my lovers, I could have you in my bed, without risking anything more. Without things getting deeper."

Clara's entire body trembled as she looked up at Zack, as she watched his face, so tired and sad. Mirroring her own, she knew.

"But they got deeper," he said, his voice rough. "And I couldn't stop it. Then I tried to reset things, and that didn't work, either. Not just because you told me where to stick it, which I absolutely deserved, but because things changed too much. Because knowing what it is to be skin to skin with you, has changed me. And it terrified me to admit that, even to myself."

"Zack…"

"You have every right to be angry at me. To hate me."

"I don't hate you."

"That's good, because it makes this next part easier. Because as terrified as I was the first time we kissed, I'm even more afraid now." He took a deep breath, his nerves visible, his control absent. "You're right, Clara Davis, you do make me tremble. You have been my friend, my partner, my lover. I want you to be all of those things to me for the rest of my life. I'll understand if you don't want the same from me. But no matter what, you have to know that I love you."

Clara felt dizzy, her fingertips numb. "You…you love me?"

"With everything. After we made love at my house, the last time, I felt like I could breathe again for the first time in fourteen years. For the first time since I lost Jake, I felt something real, something bigger than myself. Do you have any idea how much that scared me? But I realized something, the other day as I was reaching for a bottle of alcohol, to drink away the pain for the first time in fourteen years. That love can make you strong. I've always thought of it going hand in hand with loss, with weakness. But being with you…it makes me better. That's just one reason I love you so much. One of the reasons I had to tell you. Because all of my control, all of my pride, was just to cover up how scared I was. How weak I was. You've made me stronger. You've made me stop hiding."

A sob worked its way up her throat. "Zack, I thought I knew you. For seven years I thought I knew you. I thought you were this suave, together guy who had an unshakable calm that I really, really envied. And then I found out how broken you were, how messed up. I loved you before. I loved that guy I thought I knew. His jokes, his company, everything."

She pressed on, her voice cracking. "But do you want to know something? I love this man more." She stepped forward and put her palm flat on his chest, her hand unsteady. "Because this is you, and this is real. And I know you've been hurt. I know you've hurt in ways I can't imagine. And I know you aren't perfect. But you're perfect for me."

And then he was kissing her, his lips hot and hungry on hers. Her chest expanded, love, hope, filling every fiber of her body. When they parted, they were both breathing hard.

"Do you really love me?" he asked, wiping away tears she hadn't realized were on her cheeks.

"From the moment I met you."

"What a fool I was."

"I wouldn't trade the time, Zack. I wouldn't give back those years of friendship, not for anything. They made us who we are. They made us right for each other."

"I don't know if you can ever know how much your friendship has meant to me, how much your love means to me now. You're the only person I've shared myself with in so long, the only person I've wanted to share with. Without you…there would have been nothing in my life but work. You brought color, flavor."

"Cupcakes."

"That, too. And as you can see, I need someone to provide them for me because I'm useless at doing it myself. You make my life worth living, Clara. You make me better."

"I can say the same for you. I never felt beautiful, never felt special, until you."

"You're all those things. Never doubt it."

"I never will again."

"I have something for you," he said.

She smiled through a sheen of tears. "I love presents."

"I know." He reached into his pocket and pulled out a box. This one wasn't black and velvet. It was pink silk with orange blossoms. "Because you like flowers. And pink." This was for her. Only for Clara.

"I do," she said, opening the lid with shaking fingers. The ring inside was an antique style, a round diamond in the center and smaller diamonds encircling the band.

"It reminded me of you," he said. "Mostly just because it's beautiful. And so are you."

She laughed through new tears and held her hand out. "That's so lame, Zack."

"I know. It is. It's really lame. I make bad jokes sometimes, but you know that. You know everything there is to know about me, and if you can do that and love me anyway, I consider myself the luckiest man on earth."

"I do," she whispered. "Put it on me."

He took the ring out of the box and got on his knee in front of her. "Will you marry me? Clara Davis, will you be my wife, in every way. Will you understand that you are first for me, in every way. Will you love me, and let me love you?"

She wiped a tear away that was sliding down her cheek. "I will."

"And will you bake me cupcakes for as long as we both shall live?"

A watery laugh escaped her lips. "Without a walnut in sight."

He stood and kissed her on the lips. "I love you. As my friend, my future wife, my everything."

"I love you, too." She kissed him again.

"Would you mind if I stayed the night with you?" he asked, his lips hovering near hers.

"One night only?" she said, turning to him.

"No. It would never be enough. I want you every night for the rest of our lives, does that work for you?"

"Yes, Zack. I think a lifetime sounds about right."

EPILOGUE

CLARA Parsons looked at the mostly uneaten cake. Three tiers of blue frosting that had been perfectly smooth just a few hours earlier, before two, chubby hands had taken some fistfuls out of the side.

"That was the most extravagant cake I've ever seen at a one-year-old's birthday party," Zack said, looking down at the crumbs all over the kitchen floor. "And I don't think Colton ate half of it. He mostly just spread it around."

"That's what kids do, Zack."

"He's asleep. I think we put him in a sugar coma. Anyway, you only get one first birthday, I suppose. You might as well live it up."

Clara looked at the cake again. "This reminds me of another cake I made that didn't really get eaten. A wedding cake."

"I'm still very thankful that one didn't end up being used for its intended purpose."

"Oh, so am I. Because then we wouldn't have had our wedding cake, or our wedding."

"Or our son," Zack said.

"So, all things considered, it was a pretty important uneaten cake."

Zack advanced on her and pulled her up against his body, resting his forehead against hers. Her heart stopped for a moment, like it always did when she looked at him. Like it had from the moment she'd first met him.

"A lot has changed since that day," he said, dropping a kiss on her lips.

"A whole lot," she agreed.

"Do you know what's stayed the same?"

"What's that?"

"You're still my best friend."

She kissed him, deeper this time, love expanding her chest. "You're my best friend, too."

* * * * *

Mills & Boon® Hardback

May 2012

ROMANCE

A Vow of Obligation	Lynne Graham
Defying Drakon	Carole Mortimer
Playing the Greek's Game	Sharon Kendrick
One Night in Paradise	Maisey Yates
His Majesty's Mistake	Jane Porter
Duty and the Beast	Trish Morey
The Darkest of Secrets	Kate Hewitt
Behind the Castello Doors	Chantelle Shaw
The Morning After The Wedding Before	Anne Oliver
Never Stay Past Midnight	Mira Lyn Kelly
Valtieri's Bride	Caroline Anderson
Taming the Lost Prince	Raye Morgan
The Nanny Who Kissed Her Boss	Barbara McMahon
Falling for Mr Mysterious	Barbara Hannay
One Day to Find a Husband	Shirley Jump
The Last Woman He'd Ever Date	Liz Fielding
Sydney Harbour Hospital: Lexi's Secret	Melanie Milburne
West Wing to Maternity Wing!	Scarlet Wilson

HISTORICAL

Lady Priscilla's Shameful Secret	Christine Merrill
Rake with a Frozen Heart	Marguerite Kaye
Miss Cameron's Fall from Grace	Helen Dickson
Society's Most Scandalous Rake	Isabelle Goddard

MEDICAL

Diamond Ring for the Ice Queen	Lucy Clark
No.1 Dad in Texas	Dianne Drake
The Dangers of Dating Your Boss	Sue MacKay
The Doctor, His Daughter and Me	Leonie Knight

0412 GEN STD HB

ROMANCE

The Man Who Risked It All	Michelle Reid
The Sheikh's Undoing	Sharon Kendrick
The End of her Innocence	Sara Craven
The Talk of Hollywood	Carole Mortimer
Master of the Outback	Margaret Way
Their Miracle Twins	Nikki Logan
Runaway Bride	Barbara Hannay
We'll Always Have Paris	Jessica Hart

HISTORICAL

The Lady Confesses	Carole Mortimer
The Dangerous Lord Darrington	Sarah Mallory
The Unconventional Maiden	June Francis
Her Battle-Scarred Knight	Meriel Fuller

MEDICAL

The Child Who Rescued Christmas	Jessica Matthews
Firefighter With A Frozen Heart	Dianne Drake
Mistletoe, Midwife...Miracle Baby	Anne Fraser
How to Save a Marriage in a Million	Leonie Knight
Swallowbrook's Winter Bride	Abigail Gordon
Dynamite Doc or Christmas Dad?	Marion Lennox

Mills & Boon® Hardback

June 2012

ROMANCE

A Secret Disgrace	Penny Jordan
The Dark Side of Desire	Julia James
The Forbidden Ferrara	Sarah Morgan
The Truth Behind his Touch	Cathy Williams
Enemies at the Altar	Melanie Milburne
A World She Doesn't Belong To	Natasha Tate
In Defiance of Duty	Caitlin Crews
In the Italian's Sights	Helen Brooks
Dare She Kiss & Tell?	Aimee Carson
Waking Up In The Wrong Bed	Natalie Anderson
Plain Jane in the Spotlight	Lucy Gordon
Battle for the Soldier's Heart	Cara Colter
It Started with a Crush...	Melissa McClone
The Navy Seal's Bride	Soraya Lane
My Greek Island Fling	Nina Harrington
A Girl Less Ordinary	Leah Ashton
Sydney Harbour Hospital: Bella's Wishlist	Emily Forbes
Celebrity in Braxton Falls	Judy Campbell

HISTORICAL

The Duchess Hunt	Elizabeth Beacon
Marriage of Mercy	Carla Kelly
Chained to the Barbarian	Carol Townend
My Fair Concubine	Jeannie Lin

MEDICAL

Doctor's Mile-High Fling	Tina Beckett
Hers For One Night Only?	Carol Marinelli
Unlocking the Surgeon's Heart	Jessica Matthews
Marriage Miracle in Swallowbrook	Abigail Gordon

Mills & Boon® Large Print
June 2012

ROMANCE

An Offer She Can't Refuse	Emma Darcy
An Indecent Proposition	Carol Marinelli
A Night of Living Dangerously	Jennie Lucas
A Devilishly Dark Deal	Maggie Cox
The Cop, the Puppy and Me	Cara Colter
Back in the Soldier's Arms	Soraya Lane
Miss Prim and the Billionaire	Lucy Gordon
Dancing with Danger	Fiona Harper

HISTORICAL

The Disappearing Duchess	Anne Herries
Improper Miss Darling	Gail Whitiker
Beauty and the Scarred Hero	Emily May
Butterfly Swords	Jeannie Lin

MEDICAL

New Doc in Town	Meredith Webber
Orphan Under the Christmas Tree	Meredith Webber
The Night Before Christmas	Alison Roberts
Once a Good Girl...	Wendy S. Marcus
Surgeon in a Wedding Dress	Sue MacKay
The Boy Who Made Them Love Again	Scarlet Wilson

512 GEN STD LP